ALLEY KID

BRONWIN DARGAVILLE

ABOUT THE AUTHOR

BRONWIN DARGAVILLE was born in South Australia's Barossa Valley in 1976. She studied science at The University of Adelaide and The University of Queensland and has worked as a research academic in a variety of fields both in Australia and the United States. However, writing fiction has been her passion since the age of six. She has published short stories in Australia. *Alley Kid* is her first novel. Bronwin lives in Brisbane with her husband and two children.

Published in Australia by Sid Harta Publishers Pty Ltd,
ABN: 34 632 585 203
17 Coleman Parade, GLEN WAVERLEY VIC 3150 Australia
Telephone: +61 3 9560 9920, Facsimile: +61 3 9545 1742
E-mail: author@sidharta.com.au

First published in Australia 2019
This edition published 2019
Copyright © Bronwin Dargaville 2019
Cover design, typesetting: WorkingType (www.workingtype.com.au)

Dargaville , Bronwin
Alley Kid
ISBN: 978-1-925230-58-1
pp228

For my parents

CHAPTER 1

Jess glanced down the darkened hall and shivered in the silence. What if someone came along at the wrong moment? The night guard had just finished his sweep of that wing of the building. She pressed her face against the window and looked out, searching for some reassurance, but found none. Her heart was pounding. She took a deep breath and one last look down the long passage. Her fingers crept along the window sill, until they reached the latch. Slowly, she opened it, making a small click. For a moment she kept her hand cupped over the latch, as if this would stop anyone else in the building hearing the sound.

Jess looked at her watch, it was 1.20 am. She would have to hurry — in another fourteen minutes the security guard would be back. Carefully she opened the window and extracted the wire screen. A bitterly cold breeze glided into the room. She leaned a little way out of the window, her dark, pensive eyes running down the drainpipe on the side of the building until they reached the ground.

'Too far,' she whispered, but took no notice of her own observation. Quickly she shoved her small hessian backpack out of the window and let it fall to the ground, then manoeuvred herself to sit precariously on the edge of the window. Gripping tightly to the top of the window frame, she waited for a sudden gust of wind to die away, perhaps more to post-pone her next action than to decrease the danger.

She reached outside and grabbed the downpipe with one hand and edged herself out of the window. Her fingers tingled. One little slip and she would drop three stories to the ground. She had planned to close the window once she'd gone through, but that was now clearly impossible. Jess clung desperately to the damp slippery pipe. The realisation that months of careful planning and waiting had culminated and now clung perilously to a sheer brick wall began to sink into her mind. The thought caused her to pause for several seconds in an attempt to savour the moment.

Her knuckles were white, and her grip was slipping. She felt like screaming. There was no turning back. Even if she'd wanted to, she couldn't have climbed back through the window now.

Tentatively, Jess took one hand off the pipe and grabbed the window ledge beside her. She shifted her left foot to rest on a strip of metal that held the pipe to the brick wall and allowed herself to slide a little further down, until she reached the next foothold. Looking down, she could barely see the ground in the darkness. Her fingers squeaked against the tin pipe as they dragged along it.

She had reached the second storey and was able to rest her feet on the eave above the window, allowing her to relax for a moment and catch her breath. The curtains of the window were not drawn. It was Miss Brooke's office. A lamp was on dimly somewhere in the room. Jess could only see one corner of the desk from this angle but knew that Miss Brooke wasn't on duty that night. She remained pressed tightly against the wall. She couldn't be sure that none of the other night staff weren't using the office. 'Goodbye you old *bat*,' Jess whispered to the absent proprietor. She continued her slow journey to the ground. When she was, as far as she could tell, only a couple of metres away, she released her grip and dropped to the ground, landing in the dry leaves with a loud crackling thud. She leaned against the wall, trying to regain her composure.

The first time Jess had run away from home she was eight years old. It had been more of gesture than anything else but served as a kind of dress rehearsal for the years to come. Each time she seemed to get better at it and it lasted longer. But this time was different. She'd taken the train; it had been a long ride. Jess had never been on a train before and hadn't since. It had been a steep learning curve but she soon discovered ways to be inconspicuous, to protect herself, and even to get almost enough to eat. The streets of the new town became a haven, and some of the strange faces, companions. It didn't take long to adopt their hardened mentality. She'd had plenty of practice looking after herself.

Jess had been lucky; it was summer for the short time that she was one of them, with the nights warm and inviting. She didn't dare miss the few luxuries that she'd had at home — a television (although only an old black and white relic), a few books and a bicycle. She preferred not to think about the things that went along with those luxuries.

Some of the other girls would prostitute themselves. Perhaps given time, Jess would have too. The 'Alley Kids', as they were known to both themselves and the police, were a small bunch of hard-headed individuals. Most of them had homes to go back to, and did so intermittently, with only two or three being technically homeless. When it came down to it, it was everyone for himself. That was how it had been the night she was taken away by the police after an episode outside a pub. Jess had been just an onlooker, but that hadn't stopped them. She was too new to their game to know what to do when things got heated and had been the only one who hadn't managed to get away. She never saw the rest of them again. The police had brought her to Wellingwood Centre, a cross between a kind of halfway house and a juvenile detention centre, just for the night at first. That had been five months ago.

Jess picked up her bag and walked quietly through the trees, not knowing exactly where she was going. She came to the edge of the property and stepped over the low picket fence and out onto the footpath. She glanced down the length of the path in both directions. A car turned the corner into Baker Street and disappeared behind the buildings. Now everything was still and quiet, except for a trickle of water into an underground drain.

She crossed the road and began to walk through the park. The trees cast thin eerie shadows across the ground. The branches seemed to be reaching out to grab her. A sharp rustle sounded directly behind her. Jess spun around. She felt foolish as she watched a cat disappear into a clump of bushes. Its eyes shone back at her from its hiding place.

Jess continued her trek across the park. The moon, shining between the trees ahead of her, gave some faint light to see by. It seemed like a friend, beckoning her forward. Jess stopped. Across the park was a group of men, seated on motorbikes and on the ground. The sound of drunken laughter reached her. Jess stood still, watching them. She couldn't cross the park without them seeing her. Ducking behind the trees, she wove her way between them. The patch of trees came to an end and she walked through the clearing. The laughter ceased. She knew that the men were watching her. Jess waited for something to happen. Once among the trees again, she let her breath go, and couldn't help stealing a glance behind her. Everything seemed to be okay.

She came to the road and stopped at the curb. She stood there, shivering, contemplating what she'd just done. She swept her untidy black hair away from her face and walked confidently across the deserted street. She kept murmuring 'I'm free', as the realisation crept over her. It was an almost terrifying thought. Jess walked slowly over the damp grass of the nature strip at the side of the road. Everything was silent again. There were no cars, and the wind seemed to have died away. She couldn't even hear the laughter in the park from where she was. Jess felt as though the world belonged to her just then. She sat down on a stone wall, bordering a raised garden in front of a block of flats, to soak in the beauty of the night.

Jess was fourteen. She was one of the youngest kids at Wellingwood. They came from many different backgrounds and from all over the large semi-rural north of the state, since Wellingwood was the only place of its kind in the district. Some were juvenile offenders, too young for jail, and consequently the security of the place was tight. Then there were the ones like Jess, plucked from the streets by the authorities and treated basically the same due to a shortage of resources. Boys outnumbered girls by about four to one. Many of the kids were from ethnic backgrounds. Jess herself was of Latin American decent — on her mother's side at least.

Jess hated the long corridors with their gaudy orange carpet, the impersonal rows of welded steel beds, and the crowded, noisy dining halls. The place was desperately understaffed because of a lack of government funding, which meant the more demanding kids received most of the attention. Jess had just been another anonymous face. At least her parents had called her by her name. It had been almost a year since she'd seen them yet it seemed like much longer. She had no photos of them; nothing to remember them by.

Jess had a brother once, who was six years older. He was tall and wiry and tough. Most of the time he was out with his girlfriends or up to things their family never heard about. He was always looking for a new thrill. His passion for motorcycles and an obsession with speed had eventually caught up with him.

She'd watched the coffin that held his tattered body being

lowered into the earth, to rot away the remains of a prodigal life. Jess remembered their childhood days with more fondness. He used to call her 'Gypsy', a name supposedly spawned by her numerous runaway attempts and headstrong, restive nature. At times things were almost normal back then. It seemed like so long ago. Jess could even remember having a birthday party once. Her mother had made a cake and her friends had given her presents. Those days had been like a time bomb, waiting to explode. The explosion had happened long before that fateful train ride to this strange town. That was merely the gathering of the ashes. If her parents had wanted to find her, she knew they would have. If she'd wanted to go home, she knew that they realised she could have. Now the final bell of her past had tolled. They were gone and with any luck the memories would soon begin to follow.

She stared motionlessly up at the sky, its endless darkness, and the stars scattered like freckles across it. She had forgotten how beautiful it was and cherished the solitude it created. A falling star flickered for a moment across the sky. Jess drew in her breath; it was like a symbol of her freedom. The tops of the trees in front of Wellingwood seemed to touch the sky. They were even taller than the ones in the park. Jess was a safe distance from those trees and what they surrounded — for now at least.

Suddenly she felt tired. She hadn't slept at all. Her nervous energy had begun to melt into the tranquillity of the night and her eyelids became heavy. She began walking along the footpath again, toward the street light on the corner of the road. There was a bus shelter a short distance away. She reached it and sat down on the edge of the wooden seat.

Jess lay down on the hard bench, trying to find a position that was at least partly comfortable. She propped her head on her bag, containing not much more than a spare T-shirt, a light jacket and some fruit and biscuits she'd saved from breakfast that morning. A few large drops of rain began to fall, patting the cold asphalt. Jess lay there for a long time, until the rain finally sang her into a light, fitful sleep.

CHAPTER 2

The road out of town was desolate. It stretched out before her as she ambled along it. There was a row of pine trees on either side of the road, with grazing land beyond. The only movement was from Jess and a few sheep by the fence.

It was a still, clear morning. The sound of a church bell ringing in the distance somewhere behind her gave a satisfied feeling that she was leaving the town and Wellingwood behind. She didn't know where this road would take her, but it didn't really matter.

Ridgeborough was a quiet town, best known for the limestone mines and as a stop-over for the truck drivers heading north, to refuel and to get a bite to eat. Not many tourists came to Ridgeborough. They preferred the glamour and excitement of the larger towns further up the coast. Everyone seemed to know everyone here or knew someone else who did. Jess could not hide here. One night was all she could risk.

She kicked at the large white stones that lay on the side of the road, fallen from the trucks bringing them down from the quarries. The quarry road ran away to the right, then wound its way out of sight and up into the hills. It ran parallel to the highway for a distance before the trucks were able to merge with the other traffic. Each time a truck drove along it, a cloud of dust from the gravel road would first appear above the bushes. The rumble of the engine could be heard before the truck appeared around the bend, carrying its load off to some distant place. There were not many trucks that day, being Sunday.

Jess' thoughts drifted back to the people at Wellingwood. She wondered whether they knew yet that she was gone. She looked at her watch, yes, they would by now. They always began the morning rounds in the south wing, where the room was that Jess had shared with three other girls. Maybe they'd known for hours. If Nicki had woken early, she'd have gone straight to raise the alarm, Jess was sure. She knew it would have given her great satisfaction.

'Bitch,' Jess muttered, and kicked a little more aggressively at one of the stones that lay in her path. Several startled sheep scattered as it hit a fence post. The kids at Wellingwood were always talking of escaping, but not many ever made a serious attempt. The ones who did were never gone very long. It seemed that the police always knew where to look.

The others had told her she was crazy, but Jess didn't care. One day one of the other girls had found her looking out the corridor window and down to the ground below.

'You'll never get down there. You'll break your neck, and we'll have to clean up the mess,' the girl had said. There were high metal fences all around the grounds, except on the northern side, facing the street, where the front wall of the tall building served the same purpose.

It didn't matter that the road seemed to stretch out endlessly in front of her now. It would take her where she wanted to go, which was anywhere, far from Ridgborough.

* * *

The sunset glistened between the trees. Jess looked up at the sky, then down at her weary legs. Lately she'd had almost no exercise, and her body was not used to walking for hours. She sat on a rise, a short distance from the road, beneath a canopy of woodland. She sat motionless, feeling like prey that had escaped its predators. She rested her head against a tree and closed her eyes, but her mind was still active. Soon it would be dark and the idea of spending the night there under the stars held a certain appeal. She looked again at the sky, and the dark clouds that were rolling across it. The wind was picking up; it would be a rough night. The goose bumps on her skin seemed to stand out like mountains. The temperature would plummet during the night, exaggerated by the dew that would fall just before daybreak — that is, if it didn't rain.

A familiar rumble sounded over the crest in the road in the direction Jess had come. She felt the vibration of the ground beneath her as the truck appeared. It was not one of the quarry trucks, but a semi-trailer, the kind that often passed through the town.

Spontaneously, Jess got up and walked out to the edge of the road. She squinted in the glare of the headlights as the truck approached. She held out her thumb, directly in the path of the vehicle. The driver would have to slow down to avoid her, or — she hoped — he would stop.

As it neared her the truck swerved slightly. Jess turned abruptly to face it as it passed. She screamed out after it, cursing at the driver, but her voice was lost in the sound of the engine. She stood, watching it recede. But it had slowed.

Suddenly a cloud of dust went up from the rear wheels of the trailer as it verged off onto the gravel. Jess stood watching as it came to a stop. She ran towards it and came up alongside the passenger door. Since it was almost dark, she couldn't see inside, and the glass reflected her own face back at her, shining in the glow of the headlights. The window opened. The driver was leaning across the seat, looking at her.

'Sorry about that,' a husky voice said, 'I thought you were a roo, jumpin' out in front of me like that. You shouldn't do that, d'ya wanna get yourself killed or somethin'?'

Jess moved closer to the open window. 'Are you going into town?'

'Town's quite a way yet, girly. What're doing way out here anyway?'

'I just need a ride,' Jess stated plainly. He was looking at her and seemed to be making an assessment.

'Where are you heading?'

'Anywhere. Please, I just need a ride into town.'

'It ain't safe for young girls to be hitchhiking. A lot of bastards out there you know. You must be desperate.'

Jess frowned at him. He was right. She was desperate.

'Please, I'm diabetic. I have to get to a hospital, otherwise I might die,' she lied dramatically. He eyed her critically and gave a small chuckle in the back of his throat.

'Well in that case, hop in. We can't have you dying out here in the middle of nowhere.'

Jess felt briefly annoyed at the mocking tone in his voice, then cast the feeling quickly aside. She climbed into the passenger seat and slammed the door. The driver was still eying her carefully. She could see him more clearly now. His hair was cropped short. Silver-grey stubble protruded from his chin and ran up his cheekbones. There was still a hint of the deep black it had once been. Despite the grey, he looked to be in his mid-forties. He was rugged, well-built and somewhat dishevelled, looking like he'd been on the road for some time. He hit the accelerator. The truck rolled its way back onto the road and began to pick up speed. She watched him change the gears, the muscles in his forearm flexing. The gear-stick was apparently difficult to manoeuvre, but he shifted it swiftly, as he'd probably done thousands of times. The cabin of the truck was large. It was upholstered in a chestnut vinyl, although the true colour was masked by the thick film of dust that clung to it. The items littering the dashboard suggested that the vehicle was a kind of home away from home. For all she knew, it was the only home he had. There was a cigarette lighter, a half empty pack of chewing gum, a wallet and a *Penthouse* magazine. Jess had to push aside several empty bottles and beer cans before she could rest her feet on the floor.

Once out on the open road again, the driver turned his attention back to Jess. 'You're damn lucky I came along. You could've been in for a hell of a night. Them clouds don't look too friendly.'

'I would've passed out before that. My blood sugar's too high.'

'Funny that. I always thought people passed out when it was too low. I knew this chick once who was diabetic. She was always passing out, but I think she had something else the matter with her as well — lack of oxygen to the brain or something. I'm not too good with all that medical stuff. You'd have to inject yourself with somethin' wouldn't ya? What's that stuff called? I hate needles myself.'

Jess was watching the road in front of her, barely aware of his rambling. When she didn't reply, he spoke again.

'So, what's your name then?'

She hesitated, remaining silent.

'You don't have to tell me if you don't want. You can't trust these strange guys, right? I'll just call you 'Drifter'. My name's Zac. You're real pretty, you know that?' Jess squirmed uncomfortably in her seat, aware of his eyes on her.

'How old are you, Drifter?'

'What does it matter?'

'Yeah, that's what *I* reckon,' he said with a grin. He looked ahead at the road then back at Jess. 'You couldn't be much more than fifteen,' he continued. 'What's a young pretty thing like you doin' way out here anyway?' he said, repeating his earlier enquiry. Jess looked over at him. He was now watching the road again, waiting for her reply.

'I'm just going to see someone,' she said.

'A boyfriend I guess. Where does he live?'

'Why do you have to ask so many god-damn questions? I'm not asking for *your* life story.'

'Sorry. You're a feisty one, aren't you?'

Jess folded her arms over her chest and stared out the side window. It was almost completely dark now. The cloud cover brought darkness earlier than usual. The trees along the road blew about in the wind. She was glad for the warmth of the cabin, even though it smelt of cigarette smoke and unwashed clothes. She wondered which of them the second aroma came from. She decided it was definitely him. She hadn't showered for almost two days, but she figured his break from hygiene had been considerably longer. Zac's voice penetrated into her thoughts.

'You must be real stuck on him.'

'Who?'

'Your boyfriend. Coming all this way out here like this.'

'You're as nosy as hell, aren't you?' Jess shot back at him. Zac seemed to find something amusing. He chuckled to himself.

'You're not sayin' much. You got somethin' to hide? That's okay, I like mystery in a woman.' Suddenly he took a hand off the steering wheel and reached over toward her. She stiffened and drew in her breath. His hand brushed lightly over her thigh but continued past her, opening the glove box, where he took out a paper bag. 'But you're hardly a woman are you? You're just a kid.' A small smile appeared at the corner of his lips. He seemed amused at the discomfort he'd caused her. 'Do you want a doughnut?' he asked, producing a sugary ring from the paper bag. It looked like it had been there for some time. Jess shook her head. 'No of course you can't can you.' He replaced it in the bag and set it between them on the seat. 'You must be hungry though. We're almost in town. How about we grab a bite to eat? He watched her as she considered this.

She was hungry. She'd eaten nothing but her small snack supply since yesterday.

'Okay.'

The glow from the clock on the dash board indicated 8:05pm when the truck pulled into the service station on the outskirts of an unfamiliar town. Jess had no idea how far they were from Ridgeborough, but it seemed like a long way.

They went into the roadhouse, which was almost empty. There was an oily smell of fast food in the air. Jess suddenly felt ravenously hungry. A tall woman stood behind the counter. She had curly blonde hair and her makeup was thick. Jess thought it looked like she had never bothered to wash it off, but simply added another layer each day.

'Hey there, Zac. What can I get you?'

Zac gestured for Jess to take a seat at one of the tables.

'What do you want to eat?' he asked her.

She shrugged her shoulders.

'A burger and large fries, thanks, Rhonda — times two.' He seemed preoccupied with the movement of her chest beneath her skimpy top. The woman nodded and gazed critically over at Jess.

'They're getting younger and younger,' she said to Zac. Some momentary unspoken exchange seemed to take place between the two of them.

'Just get the order, Rhonda.' Zac turned back to the table where Jess was sitting.

They ate in silence. Jess watched Rhonda busying herself behind the counter. With each movement, her contours seemed to push out against the fabric of her shirt, threatening to break through. Now and then she glanced over at them.

'Shouldn't we be getting you to that hospital soon?' Zac said through a mouthful of fries.

'No,' Jess said hurriedly. 'I mean — I think I'm all right now.'

'Well ain't that amazing?'

Jess focused her eyes away from his gaze.

'Is there somewhere else I can take you then — your boyfriend?'

'No, I'll be fine.' He watched her for several moments more. Jess was glancing anxiously around the room, surveying its other occupants.

'You okay? You seem nervous, like you're expectin' someone to come in here any minute and arrest you or somethin'. What's the matter? Have you escaped from somewhere?' The question was intended as a joke, but when Jess' expression didn't change he became serious again. 'Hey, Drifter, why don't you tell me the *real* reason why you're hitchin'. Are you in some kind of trouble?'

Jess swallowed her mouthful and shot him an angry glare. 'Why don't you mind your own business!' She pushed back her chair, making a loud scraping sound against the floor.

'Thanks for the food,' she said curtly, and turned away towards the door.

'Wait. I'm sorry. No more questions, okay?'

Jess paused and looked doubtfully back at him.

'I'll take you as far as you want to go,' he said, raising his palms in front of him, as if in a truce.

She considered this for a moment. 'How far are you going?'

'Further than you'd want to go.'

'I doubt that.'

Zac drove in silence, concentrating on the road or some distant thoughts. Jess had begun to relax a little. Her stomach was full, and every moment took her further from her enemies. She rested her head against the door, allowing her eyes to fall closed. It had been a long day and sleep threatened to enclose her.

Jess didn't know how long she'd been dozing when she felt the truck slowing and the wheels rolling over the bumpy gravel on the side of the road. She straightened up in her seat. 'What are you doing? Why are you stopping?' She could barely see Zac in the darkness of the cabin. All she could make out was his outline.

'A man's gotta sleep some time, don't he?'

'I guess,' Jess said sleepily, sinking back into her position against the window, satisfied with this reply.

The cabin rocked as Zac opened the door and heaved himself to the ground. The icy air floated inside, making her shiver.

In a few moments he returned. He tilted his seat forward, revealing a small doorway behind it.

'What's that?'

'It's the sleeping compartment. Most trucks this size have 'em.' He manoeuvred his large body awkwardly inside it.

A few minutes later Jess was startled by a hand on her shoulder.

'Wanna come in here, it's much more comfortable?'

'No,' she said quickly, squirming away from his touch. 'I can sleep here.'

'Come on. You can sleep in here and I'll stay out front. That way I can keep an eye on things — in case anybody comes.'

Jess thought that this seemed unlikely, but she was too tired to argue. He was right — it was more comfortable, and the bed was soft. It didn't take long for her to fall asleep.

CHAPTER 3

Sometime during the night Jess was woken suddenly by movement in the cabin. She opened her eyes. It was a moment or two before she saw him in the darkness. He was crouched just inside the door of the compartment where she slept, wearing only his jeans. His bare chest looked shiny and damp with perspiration and the muscles were prominent beneath his darkly tanned skin. Around his neck was a chain, with a gold bullet hanging from it that swung like a pendulum as he leaned slightly forward. He had a tattoo on his left pectoral, but Jess couldn't make out what it was. Suddenly he spoke.

'Don't you think it's time you repaid me for my hospitality — letting you use my truck and all that?' He sounded cool and composed, as though he'd been awake for hours.

Jess tried to sit up, herself suddenly wide awake. 'I haven't got any money.'

Zac gave a hoarse laugh that seemed to ripple from somewhere deep in his throat. 'I wasn't talking about money.'

A bolt of fear shot through her. He began to move inside the compartment.

'I don't think this thing was made for two people,' she said weakly, shrinking back against the far wall of the tiny space. He laughed again.

'I've always been one to break the rules.' He moved closer

to her. 'Even at school, I was a bad boy. I bet ya don't know what the girls used to call me?'

Jess's mind spun, as he left this question open to her imagination. She wondered fleetingly whether she was dreaming. He was looking down at her now, not speaking, just looking with his steely grey eyes. His large form hovered directly above her as she tried to hunch herself further into the corner. He dropped forward onto all fours. His knees straddled her, stretching the blanket tight over her stomach. Panic began to rise in her. He was blocking the exit. She straightened her arms in front of her to stop him getting any closer, but he was too strong.

'Didn't I tell you it was part of the deal? I must have forgotten.'

She felt him lower himself onto her. His bullet touched her skin. It was cold, like an icicle and sent a shiver through her. She felt the hair on his chest brush over her. She tried to pull her shirt up close around her neck, but his hand slid down inside, over the front of her shoulder. His touch sent cold shock waves through her body. She scrunched her eyes tightly closed and shook her head from side to side, trying to deny the reality of what was happening. He had lured her right where he wanted her. *How could she have been so stupid?* How could she have thought this stranger would get her away from the life and the people she hated? He was just one of them.

His bristly face scraped over her neck, then she felt his lips touch her skin below the jaw. He exhaled deeply. His hot breath on her neck repulsed her. She reeled at his smell.

A surge of anger rushed through her. She began to scream.

'Get off me!' She struggled against him, but she could hardly move. His enormous weight felt like it was crushing her. Terror gripped her. He could do anything to her — anything. One of her arms was pinned against the wall but the other was free. She began to pound his back with her fist, but he seemed to barely feel it. She scraped her rough nails over his skin. He cursed at her. She ignored it and kept screaming.

'You *arsehole*! Get the hell *off* me!'

Just then she caught sight of something wedged between the bed and the wall that faced the back of the driver's seat. She pushed the blanket aside with one foot. It was a first-aid kit and beside it was an open tool box. In an instant her free hand lurched towards it, grabbing the first object that it touched.

With a fierce burst of fury, she drove it hard into the side of Zac's head, which was just centimetres from her own. She heard him cry out in pain as her weapon connected with his temple. She drew it back again and rammed it repeatedly against him. He tried to grab her arm but missed the moving target. She felt his grip on her weaken, then finally he went limp, sinking onto the bed. She threw down the object and struggled out from under his body.

Out of breath, she scrambled through the tiny trap door and onto the front seat. She looked back at the hulk of a body that lay awkwardly against the back wall. Blood ran in a thin stream from his forehead and the scratches on his back. She didn't know whether he was dead or alive, and just then she didn't care.

Turning her back on him, she reached towards the two-way radio and picked up the hand-piece. With a shaking hand she pressed her thumb against the send button and almost shouted into the receiver.

'Can anybody hear me?' Her voice came out in a choked distorted sound. 'Help! Please help me! Can anyone hear me?' she cried, this time louder. She released the button and listened. All she heard was the static through the speaker and her own heavy breathing. There *had* to be somebody out there. She spoke into the receiver again. When there was no reply, she threw the hand-set viciously against the dashboard and collapsed against the seat.

After a moment or two the background noise cut out and a clear male voice came over the radio. Jess reached quickly for the receiver.

'A guy attacked me — I think I might have killed him — please help me!'

The voice replied immediately. 'Okay, calm down. Where are you?'

'Somewhere out of Lachlin Creek, by the road. I don't know how far.'

'Which side of the town? Ridgeborough?'

'No, the other side.'

'Okay, just stay there.'

Jess dropped the radio. The fear had subsided slightly. Someone was coming. Her eyes flashed quickly across the cabin and settled on Zac's wallet, which was still on the dashboard. She picked it up and opened it. There were several twenty-dollar notes inside. She stuffed them quickly into her pocket, then opened the driver's door and jumped to the ground. She slammed the door behind her. If Zac came around, she could not let him find her.

Jess had a clear view of the road from where she was, crouched in a carpet of wet leaves and moss. It was not raining, but it had been sometime earlier in the night. Every now and then, a large droplet fell from the branches of the trees above her head. The ones that landed on her skin sent a cold tingle through her, the way Zac's bullet had done. She sat there, trembling, from shock or anger or a combination of both. She could still smell him on her clothes — that rank, vile smell. She could not rid herself of the terrible feeling it created. It seemed like hours that she sat there, frozen by the thoughts of what he'd done to her and by the chilling wind. It was just the same as always, only this time it was worse. Her father's face appeared before her eyes and merged with the face of her new assailant.

Jess could see the truck, a safe distance away, parked in the bay and facing her. There was no movement, no sign of life. She felt a new fear grip her. What if she *had* killed him?

An insect crawled over her leg. She swiped at it. From above her in the trees, an owl began to hoot. The dark lonely night surrounded her. Soon someone would be here. What would she tell them? The man on the radio sounded composed and business-like. What did she expect him to do — tell her that everything would be all right and then to let her be on her way, running from the police and whoever else they had after her? She began to wish she hadn't called for help — people would just ask questions and then turn her in. How could she be sure it wasn't just another creep like Zac? She looked around at the darkness, but there was nowhere to go. She was in the middle of nowhere.

After what seemed like a long time, the glow of car headlights appeared along the highway. A car pulled slowly into the parking bay and came to a stop in front of the truck. Jess froze. It was a police car.

'It looks like this is it,' she heard a voice say.

She slowly lowered herself closer to the ground until she was lying on her stomach. Two police officers got out of the car and walked over to the truck. One of them began looking around outside. His eyes scanned the trees, past Jess's hiding place, then he walked around to the back of the truck. The other officer opened the door and looked inside. Jess saw a torch beam flick jerkily around the cabin. Her heart was in her mouth. The officer called out suddenly to his partner.

'There's a man in here. I don't know where the girl is, but it looks like she attacked him with a screwdriver. Hopefully she's still around here somewhere.' He looked over again at the trees and began towards them. 'This guy's going to need an ambulance.' The first officer walked back to the patrol car.

Jess shrunk backward. The twigs cracked under her body. She grimaced. He had surely heard it.

'Is there anyone there? We're here to help you. You'd better come out.'

Jess's mind was locked in a terrible numbness. What could she do? She hesitated. They would take her back to Wellingwood. *No!* Despite the cold, she began to sweat. The thought paralysed her. She could never go back to that place.

He was looking directly at her now.

'You have to come out. We need to talk to you. It's okay,' he coaxed gently. Jess slowly raised her head.

'Hey, Steve, I've found her,' he called over his shoulder.

Jess sat up and waited for him to approach. She stood up slowly as he took her arm. Her legs had gone to sleep after being in the same position for so long.

'Did you call for help?'

Jess nodded.

'Are you all right?'

She nodded again, this time looking him straight in the face. She couldn't see his eyes because the brim of his hat cast a shadow over them, but she knew he was looking intently at her. She collected herself to speak.

'Yeah, I'm okay,' she said, but didn't think she'd convinced him. He held her by the arm. Was he expecting her to run?

They were joined by the other officer. In the dark the two of them looked almost identical in their uniforms and hats. They addressed her with twin stares.

'Is he dead?' Jess asked in a monotone.

'No, not yet.' The officer who had spoken turned to his partner. 'The guy's pretty bad. I've got an ambulance on its way out here. Is she okay?' he said, as if Jess wasn't capable of answering for herself.

'I think so.'

He turned to Jess.

'Are you injured at all?'

'No.'

'Can you tell me what happened?'

Jess hesitated. 'Um, no — I mean, don't I have the right to remain silent or something?'

'You're not under arrest. We're not trying to incriminate you just now.'

'Like hell! I've just nearly killed a guy.' The fear rippled through her voice as it rose in volume.

'Did he attack you?'

She looked at the ground.

'That's what you said over the radio.'

'I wasn't thinking straight, I was just scared.' She wanted to keep things as simple as possible.

'So, you're telling me that you decided to stab a guy in the head with a screwdriver in the middle of nowhere for no rea-son whatsoever?' His voice was calm. There was a moment's pause. 'That doesn't look too good for you, does it?'

'Yes, he attacked me,' Jess rushed, realising the trap she'd gotten herself into. 'But I don't feel like talking about it, it was so awful.' She dropped her head in the pose of a deeply distraught victim. The truth was that most of the initial shock had melted away. She'd been abused too many times to allow it to turn her into a nervous wreck, but the action had the desired effect.

The first officer cut in, 'She's in shock. Why don't we con-tinue this back at the station? It's cold out here.'

His companion nodded. 'I'll wait here with the bloke; the ambulance should be here soon.'

Jess was guided into the back of the patrol car. They had her. She stared miserably ahead. The door slammed shut and she was trapped.

CHAPTER 4

The police station smelled of paper, ink and disinfectant. The front of the station was empty except for another uniformed figure, a youngish-looking woman who sat behind the desk. She was on the phone. The officer who'd brought Jess in went over to her and spoke quietly. She looked Jess over, while listening at the receiver. She raised her eyebrows and gestured something to him.

Jess felt like a criminal in a movie. The only thing missing was the handcuffs. This police station wasn't like the ones in the movies though. Those were always buzzing with activity, even at this hour of the night. This one was quiet. It was an old building and the furniture was a similar age. Several framed certificates hung in a row along the back wall.

Jess was told to sit on a chair by the desk and wait. On the wall opposite was a large photograph of the local police band, winning an award at some kind of festival. The whole place was quite disappointing. If she had to be hauled into a police station in the middle of the night, it could at least have been an interesting one.

After a few minutes, the male officer returned and ushered her through a door with the words: INTERVIEW ROOM painted on it. He closed it behind him and indicated for Jess to take a seat on one side of a large table. He'd brought her backpack in with him and put it down on the floor. Jess's eyes followed it automatically. It looked like it had been opened and searched since it wasn't properly closed. The officer sat down opposite her.

'Okay.' The constable tried to get comfortable in the wooden chair. One leg seemed to be shorter than the rest. Jess had clearly gotten the better deal of the two chairs in the room. 'Let's start with something simple,' he continued. 'What's your name?'

Jess remained motionless, staring at the table top, bare except for a laptop computer in front of the constable.

'Well, kid, what's your name?'

'What's yours?'

'Ronald. Call me Ron. Now how about you?'

Jess looked up at him and eyed him squarely. He had removed his hat, revealing a partly bald head and a pair of sharp interrogative eyes. She avoided making contact with them as she said, 'Jennifer. Call me Jen.'

'Okay, Jen, that's a start. Where do you live?'

'Nowhere around here,' she said, biting on a finger nail and casting a careful look at him.

'Where are your parents?'

'I haven't got any parents.'

'You must have a foster home then? Someone who looks after you?'

'I look after myself, I'm not a kid.'

The policeman nodded slowly.

'How old are you then, exactly?' he queried.

'How old are *you*?'

'Fifty-five.'

Jess looked down at the table again. He waited for her response. After a while Jess spoke, simply to break the silence.

'I'm sixteen.'

He nodded again.

'Would you like to tell me what happened tonight? Do you know who the man in the truck was?'

She stiffened at his use of the past tense. 'He said his name was Zac.'

'Is he a friend of yours?'

'No.'

'What were you doing with him then? Were you hitch-hiking?'

Jess remained silent.

'It's all right. You can talk to me. Nothing's going to happen to you.'

'It's all pretty hazy, it just happened so fast, you know what I mean?' she said evasively.

'Can't you at least give me some kind of general outline of what took place?' he said patiently. Jess shook her head.

'I understand you may have been through a lot, but you have to tell me what this man did to you to make you do what you did.'

'Can I have some water?'

'Yeah, good idea, I need something too.'

He rose from his seat and disappeared out the door. In a moment he returned and handed Jess a glass. He rested a cup of coffee on his own side of the table.

'Any more requests?'

'Yes. Can I have a lawyer?'

'You may not need one yet.'

'Am I going to be charged?' Jess asked quizzically.

'How can I answer that if you won't tell me what happened? You're only hurting yourself.'

Jess thought this was just a ploy to make her talk. She suddenly decided she would tell him, even if only to make sure Zac got what he deserved.

She began to recount, unemotionally, what had happened since Zac had picked her up, until the time she'd called for help. Ron leaned back in his chair.

'All right, let's go over this one more time. You were hitching, and this guy — Zac — picked you up about 6 pm. You travelled with him in his truck for several hours.'

'I didn't look at the time, I'm not sure of it.'

Ron continued. 'He bought you some food at a road house along the way. Sometime later he stopped at the parking bay and told you to get into the sleeping compartment. You wouldn't, so he tried to force you. He began assaulting you. You made it clear you wanted him to stop, but he didn't. That's when you reached for the screwdriver and attacked him with it.'

Jess nodded her head. It was the truth, or close enough. If she told him she'd voluntarily gotten inside the sleeping compartment he might think she'd asked for it. She'd been watching him type all the details into the computer in front of him. He looked satisfied with the information. He addressed her again.

'Why were you hitch-hiking? You must have known that's a pretty dangerous thing to do?'

Jess didn't feel like a lecture. She didn't say anything, but simply continued to stare at the table.

'All right, you don't have to tell me that right now, but I need to know of someone who I can contact, someone you live with perhaps. Somebody must be worried sick about you.'

Jess watched the steam rising from the cup of coffee in his hand, poised below his chin. It swirled in front of his face, reminding her of a TV show she'd seen once, where a monster emerged from a steaming mud pool.

'Nobody worries about me. Nobody gives a shit, and neither do you!' she spat accusingly at him. Ron put his coffee down on the table and leaned forward.

'Jen, you have to cooperate, you need to answer the questions.'

Jess had no intention of cooperating. She was getting restless and wanted to get out of this place. She glanced around the room which was becoming stuffy.

'This job must be the pits,' she said.

'It has its moments.'

He watched her for a few more seconds, then stood up. He was getting restless too, or else he wasn't finding the chair comfortable. He paced over to the far wall, stroking his chin, as if wondering what to do next. For a moment he seemed to be studying a chart on the wall, but apparently not taking anything in. He turned back to face her abruptly, as if this act in itself would produce the desired response. When it didn't, he walked over to Jess's chair. He knelt down on one knee as if reasoning to a child and spoke slowly.

'Why don't you tell me who you *really* are?'

'You're the cop, *you* figure it out.'

'Listen kid, it's too late at night to start getting cute. Let's just cut the crap shall we, so we can both get out of here? My shift's up in ten minutes.' Jess thought that explained his continual glancing at his watch.

'What's the time?' Jess inquired. She didn't care what the time was. All she wanted was for them to leave her alone.

'It's 2:22 *am.*' He emphasised the am.

'Eight minutes.'

'What?'

'Your shift finishes in eight minutes, that is, unless you finish at 2:32.' Jess listened to herself ramble. Perhaps she was just trying to avoid answering the questions. She didn't know. She was tired. The events of the last twenty-four hours were swarming around in her head so that she could barely separate them.

Just then there was a knock on the door. Ron stood up and opened it.

'Stay here for a moment,' he commanded after a short, hushed exchange with the policewoman. He picked up his coffee and left the room, closing the door behind him. Jess let her head rest on the table. The muscles in the back of her neck were aching.

A few minutes later, Ron returned. He spoke to her in a

brisk business-like voice now, not even bothering to return to his seat.

'It's interesting — you turning up like this. I've just been given a description of a girl reported missing from Wellingwood Detention Centre this morning — dark hair; olive skin; slight build; tall for a fourteen-year-old.'

Jess raised her head stiffly.

'I told you I was sixteen.'

'Your little game is over Jessica — Jessica Dimitri.' He stated her name triumphantly.

'You can't prove anything. I don't have any ID.'

Ron cocked his head back, almost in amusement. 'I don't have to prove anything. You wouldn't find too many such young ladies roaming around a place like this. They'll recognise you at the centre anyway,' he shrugged.

'No!' Jess sat up straight to face him. Her eyes were wide, suddenly animated. 'I'm *not* going back there.'

'Yes, you are.' His tone was decisive. Jess put a hand to her face. She felt the blood rushing to it.

'I'm not going back,' she repeated.

'Why not?' He said with a calmness that annoyed her.

'It sucks. It's like hell. It's a prison. And I haven't done anything wrong!' She stood up, bringing herself closer to his level.

'We get some pretty good reports of the place.'

'Yeah, you would.' Jess's voice was raised now, for the first time since she'd been there.

'There's nowhere else for you to go for now. There are processes to go through.'

Jess fought back the tears. The only place where she was wanted was basically a jail, and only because having a runaway would make them look bad. How could she go back to a place where she was just another number on their records, just another face in the queue at mealtimes? How could she explain this to these people who had comfortable homes and a nice family to greet them when they came home, tired after a long day?

'Please! Don't send me back there. You don't know what it's like.' She was pleading now, and feeling so dizzy that she found it necessary to grab hold of the back of the chair for support. *She could not go back!*

The door opened and the policewoman came in. She folded her arms and looked at Jess. From her expression it was impossible to tell what she was thinking, but she'd obviously been listening to the drama.

'But there you're with other kids your own age, your friends,' Ron continued.

'I hate them,' Jess said flatly. She kicked viciously at the table leg. It stung her toe. The woman walked over to her and put an arm around Jess's shoulders. It was tossed aside roughly. The woman seemed unfazed. Ron had taken off his glasses and was rubbing his eyes.

'You poor thing,' she said sympathetically to Jess.

'She has to go back to Wellingwood,' Ron said, as if his colleague didn't realise this.

'Well let's not wake anyone up tonight,' she said.

'What are you suggesting we do with her then?'

'Why don't you lock me up here? That's what you do with criminals, isn't it?'

They ignored her.

'You're finished for the night, aren't you? Why don't you take her home with you? Bring her back in the morning, it's only for a few hours,' the policewoman suggested. She and Ron exchanged glances. Ron looked doubtfully at Jess, then back at the woman.

'You've got to be kidding!'

'We can't keep her here. She needs some sleep. She's just a kid.'

You don't know anything about kids, Jess thought. Or maybe she did.

Ron scratched his head, looking awkward. He looked once more at his watch. He seemed to be considering this option carefully.

'Well I guess ...' he began.

'Shirley won't mind, will she?' The woman had clearly decided that Jess was harmless. In a way this annoyed her, but in another way, she felt glad. She was standing silently, listening to them decide her fate. The policewoman turned to Jess.

'How would you like to go home with Constable West tonight?'

Jess shrugged her shoulders. Anything was better than Wellingwood, even sleeping in a cop's house.

'Sounds like it's arranged,' Ron said reluctantly.

Jess waited by the front desk while he gathered his things together. She was sure that this kind of thing could only happen in such a small town. She followed him to his car which was parked by the side of the building. She climbed into the new-looking Commodore. It swung out of the car park and onto the road.

'So, Jessica.'

'It's Jess.'

'So, Jess, do you like old farm houses?'

'Not really.'

Ron glanced sideways at her.

'You can sleep in the spare room tonight. We save it for when our son comes home. It's probably full of guy's stuff, but you won't mind, will you?'

'Am I going to be charged?'

'I doubt it. The law looks pretty kindly on victims of sexual assault, especially if they're under age. Of course, we have to get Zac's side of the story first — when he wakes up.'

'What if he doesn't wake up?'

'You'd better hope he wakes up. It'll be more serious for you if he doesn't.' His expression was unchanging as he watched the road in front of him.

'Great. My word against a dead man's.'

'He's not dead yet.'

'He might be.'

'Let's just take it as it comes, shall we, huh?' Jess sensed him trying to brighten her mood.

'That's easy for you to say. You're not the one who could

be up for murder and spend the rest of your life in a prison cell,' she said mournfully.

'I doubt it will come to that. Anyway, you're a minor. It wouldn't be a real jail, just a remand centre, for juvenile offenders.'

'Like Wellingwood?'

'I guess.'

Jess shrugged.

'Then I don't care what happens. No matter what, it'll be the same,' she said dramatically.

Ron looked over at her. She had a stony expression on her face.

'Hey, I'm sure everything will be all right,' he assured her. There was no response from his passenger.

For a while they travelled in silence, then Jess said, 'I've never been to a cop's house before.'

'It's not so different. We're human too you know. We're not from another planet.'

Jess didn't reply.

'We've got a bit of land out of town. We thought it would be a nice place to retire one day. Where did you live before you went to Wellingwood?'

'Don't you cops *ever* stop asking questions?' Her voice projected hostility.

'Damn touchy aren't you?'

They drove the rest of the way in silence. It wasn't far. The car rolled up the long driveway of the small rural property and stopped in an open garage. Ron led her across a neat yard to the house. Before he opened the door, Ron turned to her.

'Ssh. My wife's probably asleep.' He took her straight to the spare room.

'Get some sleep. We'll both need to be thinking straight tomorrow.' Before turning and closing the door, he added, 'I hope you'll be comfortable.'

Jess suddenly realised how tired she was. She went over to the bed and folded back the quilt. She eased her tense, stiff body onto it. She closed her eyes and sunk into the soft mattress. In a few minutes she was asleep.

Shirley West moved efficiently around the small kitchen. Jess watched her from where she sat at the table. Shirley glided from the fridge to the bench, then over to the stove where she was making scrambled eggs. She gave them a hefty stir and turned back to the bench to continue chopping some bacon. Shirley was a robust woman of ample proportions. She wore a light-yellow tracksuit beneath a floral apron. She was energetic and bouncy, despite her size — the kind of woman who could do quite a few things at once.

Jess tried to remember the last time she'd been inside a proper house. It was probably her parents' house. It was nothing like this though. Her mother wouldn't be bustling around the kitchen. She'd still be in bed, sleeping off the effects of whatever she'd been doing the night before. Jess would always get her own breakfast, add her dishes to the growing pile of unwashed plates and empty tin cans and go off to school. If she ever slept in, no one would wake her. She'd just miss a lesson or two. She remembered one day when the principal had come to the house to talk to her parents about her constant lateness, after getting no response from numerous notes sent home. Her mother had been out with one of her many male acquaintances, and her father was drunk after one of their rows. Jess shuddered at the memory.

She watched Shirley busying herself with the breakfast preparation. She was taken in by her enthusiasm. She was clearly enjoying having someone to fuss over. That morning Jess had stayed under the shower for a long time, perhaps longer than would have been polite, but she didn't care. The hot water running over her body felt wonderful. She'd stood there with her eyes closed, thinking of how good it was to be this far from Wellingwood, if only for a short time.

Shirley placed a large steaming plate of scrambled eggs and bacon in front of her — it looked glorious. Shirley stood back and watched with satisfaction as Jess devoured her specialty.

'Do you like it? There's more in the pan still. We need to fatten you up.'

'I'm not staying here,' Jess said, as much to keep herself from feeling too much at home as to remind Shirley.

'Ah well, while you're here you won't starve, I can tell you that. No one in my house goes hungry. I dare say you wouldn't get good home-cooked meals where you're from. Ronald tells me that you lived at some kind of refuge home. That's no way for anyone to grow up, I say.'

'You try telling *them* that. They get off on making people's lives miserable. They're sending me back there you know.'

'A kid your age should be out having fun with your friends. When I was young all I wanted was to meet Mr Right, get married and have babies. Before you know it, you're tied down with a family and don't have time to have fun. Do it while you can, that's what I say.' She shuffled the remaining eggs around in the pan.

'Nobody has any fun at Wellingwood. They just get bored. And cry a lot.'

'Poor things.' Shirley looked pityingly at her. 'It must be awful. It makes you want to go in there and rescue them all.' She said, hugging herself in a mock embrace.

Jess watched her, making sure the woman looked sufficiently distraught, then said,

'You could let me stay here.' Her tone was matter of fact and the statement a simple one.

Shirley sank her large body down into a chair alongside Jess and looked at her seriously. 'I really wish I could.'

'You can.'

'I don't think Ron would like it.'

'He doesn't like *me* you mean.'

'No, that's not what I mean. Dear, I'd love to have you ... but it's difficult ... you know ... just difficult.'

Jess looked back down at her empty plate.

'Do you want some more?'

Jess shook her head. For a few moments, neither of them spoke.

'Why don't you see if they'll let somebody foster you? You know, a family?'

It took a moment for Jess to react to this. She frowned. 'Some of the kids from Wellingwood got foster homes. They never came back.'

'That must mean it worked out all right.'

'I guess.'

Shirley got up. She walked over to Jess and put an arm around her, the way the policewoman had done. This time Jess did not pull away. She quite liked Shirley.

'Don't worry, I'll make sure they find you a nice home,' she said gently. Jess shook her head again.

'There's too many kids. People only want the cute ones.' She spoke with a hardened realism. Jess didn't allow herself to dream.

'I'll get Ron to look into it this morning when he takes you back to the station.' Shirley obviously didn't share Jess's views. She looked at Jess with an intensity that Jess could not have imagined from this breezy woman. 'I won't let them take you back to that place,' she said.

CHAPTER 5

Jess stepped up to the wood-veneer front door, which was peeling at the edges. She was still trying to come to terms with the events of the morning. Shirley had been insistent that they call the Department of Family and Community Services. She was adamant and eventually the phone call had been made. The news had not been good. There was a waiting list for foster homes and only those labelled 'critical' were given priority. But, they were told, the request would be passed on to the relevant division for processing in the usual way.

Ron drove Jess back to the police station at around ten o'clock. After a session of exhaustive questioning, and no further news on Zac, there was a phone call from the department. It was all like a whirlwind to Jess. She couldn't remember much of what they'd told her, only that due to the delicate nature of the circumstances, she was better off in a private arrangement, at least until things were sorted out and any charges had been laid. Nobody mentioned whether those charges were against her or Zac. They said something about giving her an emergency placement and that she was lucky they'd found somewhere. Jess didn't feel lucky. She felt as though her life was dangling from the end of a thread hanging from the top of a cliff, with a raging torrent below. Everything was happening so fast. She hadn't had much time to think.

Now she was standing on the front porch of this house, fighting hard to control the jumble of emotions racing around inside her. An employee from the department stood beside her. The woman stepped up to ring the doorbell, then back to be level with Jess.

Presently, another woman appeared behind the screen door. Her face lit up with a smile when she saw them. The two women greeted each other warmly. They were evidently not strangers. Jess realised there would have been rigorous screening of this potential foster family before today, as well as a lot of paperwork and planning.

'This is Jess, Mrs Pullin,' Jess's companion announced. They were not on first name terms though, Jess noticed.

'Hi,' she said nervously, managing a small smile. The truth was she was terrified. She didn't know what she would think of them. She didn't know what they would think of her.

'Come on in,' Mrs Pullin grinned, opening the door and stepping aside to let them through.

'You'll stay for a cuppa, won't you?' Mrs Pullin asked the social worker with a hopeful expression as they stepped inside. They walked down a dark hallway and through the kitchen door at the other end. A bronze-coloured Dachshund appeared from one of the rooms. It sniffed at Jess's shoes, then trotted after its owner.

'Olivia, come in here,' Mrs Pullin called through the open sliding glass doors that revealed part of the living room, from where a television blared incessantly. She turned back to them.

'Now, would you like some coffee?' she offered cheerfully to Jess's companion. 'A soft drink Jess?'

She declined, and as she sat at the table watching the women, she remembered what it was like to live in a family. She felt uncomfortable in this home which was supposed to be hers, a least for a while. Mrs Pullin cast her attention toward the living room again for a moment.

'Olivia, I said come in here, Jess is here.' There was no reply. Jess thought she noticed a look of annoyance flicker briefly across her face before turning pleasantly back to them. Jess watched Mrs Pullin carefully, trying to imagine what she was going to be like. Already, she could tell that she was a fussy woman, and perhaps a little nervy, though she was friendly and talkative. She kept the conversation going with her cheery small talk. Jess didn't join in. She sat watching, but barely listening.

Mrs Pullin was slim and wore a full white skirt and floral blouse. Her hair was curly, and a light brown colour. It was pulled back in a fluffy mass. Her face was flushed and transpired a flurried disposition. Your average nineteen sixties housewife, Jess thought, remembering some TV re-runs from that era. The image fit well.

When the social worker had gone, Jess felt the panic return. Now everything even vaguely familiar was gone. Mrs Pullin cleared away the coffee mugs and deposited them in the sink. She showed Jess into the living room. A girl of about sixteen lay on the couch, her eyes glued to the television screen.

'Olivia, I'd like you to meet Jess.' The girl looked up from the television for a moment. Her eyes moved over Jess, and then without uttering a word she turned back to the soap opera she'd been watching. The smile had vanished from her mother's face.

'*Please* make Jess feel welcome,' Mrs Pullin said, in a somewhat pleading tone. Jess sensed a certain friction between them.

From somewhere within the rooms of the house a phone began to ring. Mrs Pullin disappeared. Jess was left alone with Olivia and the boisterous characters on the TV screen. She stood by the door for a minute or two. When Olivia continued to ignore her, she sat herself down in an arm chair, and propped her chin on her hands.

Olivia looked graceful and had long brown hair that fell over her shoulder. Her features were soft and defined and outlined with perhaps a more than appropriate amount of makeup. Jewellery decorated almost every exposed part of her body. She was dressed in light green cotton pants, a white T-shirt, and matching green braces over her shoulders. She lay on her stomach with the remote control in her hands.

'It must be captivating,' Jess finally said, sensing a thinly-veiled hostility and matching it with her own. The girl swivelled her head in a smooth motion to look at her.

'What!' she snapped, screwing up her previously smooth, crease-free face. Jess stared at her for a few seconds, taunting her.

'What you're watching. It must be really good if you're just going to lie there all day in front of the box.'

'Who says I'm going to lie here all day, and what business is it of *yours*?' Olivia shot back, her tone becoming defensive.

Jess gave a short laugh.

'And what's so funny?' Olivia asked bitterly. Jess focused her eyes narrowly on the hostile stranger. Their eyes locked on each other for several moments. A pang of immediate dislike flickered through Jess. Instead of answering, she turned her back on her and stalked out of the room, pausing briefly in the doorway.

'You'd better keep watching — wouldn't want to miss anything.'

Once out of the room, Jess took a deep breath. 'Whoa!' she mouthed silently to herself. This was going to be interesting.

At dinner time, Olivia chatted cheerfully to her mother, and every now and then shot a brief glance at Jess, who was eating her food in silence. Jess had been wondering where Mrs Pullin's husband was. That is, if she had one. She listened to the conversation, trying to find out information about these strangers.

When dinner was over, Jess ventured into what was known as the sitting room, at the front of the house. It was a cosy looking room, with a fireplace and fur rugs on the carpet. She wandered slowly around the room, looking at the photographs and ornaments which had seemingly been arranged with great care. Jess found a photo of Olivia when she had been in primary school, smiling sweetly up at her. There was a black and white photo of an old woman, sitting in a garden, and one of a couple at their wedding, showered in confetti. Jess thought it must have been Mrs Pullin and her husband. She picked it up and looked at it for several moments before replacing it on the mantelpiece.

When Mrs Pullin found her, she was gazing out of the window into the street.

'What are you thinking about?' she asked Jess kindly.

'Nothing much,' Jess answered, with equal politeness as before, not wanting to reveal her true thoughts.

'Sit down,' Mrs Pullin said. Jess obediently sat.

'It must be hard for you to come to a new home where you don't know anyone,' she began. Jess remained silent, waiting for her to go on.

'I just hope you can make yourself feel at home here. We want you to be part of the family.'

'I don't think that daughter of yours feels the same way,' Jess replied, fiddling with a thread on the sofa.

'Oh Olivia, she'll be all right,' she assured her off-hand-edly. Jess raised her eyebrows, as if in disbelief, but she didn't care about Olivia.

'If you ever want to talk to someone, I'm here for you, you know that don't you?' she told Jess gently, sounding like the actor from the TV shows she'd reminded Jess of earlier. 'I know what you must have been through.'

'No, you don't!' Jess's voice became sharp. Mrs Pullin must have realised she'd hit a nerve, and seemed about to change the subject, when Jess suddenly asked the question that had been on her lips since dinner.

'Why did you want a foster kid, Mrs Pullin?'

'You can call me Margi, okay,' she smiled. 'We wanted to help someone, give them a second chance. We only have one child, and plenty of bedrooms,' was her explanation.

'Oh,' Jess squeaked, not knowing what to feel or think.

After acquainting her with a few house rules, Margi left Jess alone again. She felt strange in this foreign room, full of family closeness. She felt as though she did not belong, in this room, or with these people.

That night in her new bedroom, Jess tossed and turned. It wasn't the bed. She'd slept in so many different beds that she'd gotten used to them all having their own characteristics. She was feeling listless and found herself wishing she was somewhere else, but then again, she'd been doing that a lot lately.

After what seemed like a long time of restless tossing about, Jess let her eyelids fall open again. She glanced across the room to the open window where a small alarm clock sat on the sill, the colon between the numerals flashing steadily. The moonlight fell on the shining luminescent LED numbers, seeming to double their brightness. 12.30 am. Jess flopped back onto her pillow. She lay on her back, thinking of how slowly the time seemed to pass at night when you are awake.

Just as she lay still, and was finally drifting off to sleep, the sound of raised voices became loud in her ears. For a few minutes she stayed there and listened, catching only the odd word. She could hear a man's voice, raised and angry, and a woman's, pleading and distraught. Jess pushed the quilt aside and slid out of bed. She went over to the door and pressed her ear against it. Still, she couldn't make out what was going on. She opened the door a fraction. It creaked on its hinges. Jess peeped out. All she could see was the dim hall and the banisters of the stairs. Opening the door fully she could hear every word.

'What is wrong with you woman?'

'What is wrong with *me*? I'll tell you what is damn well wrong with me. You come bursting in here after midnight, totally off your face. Where have you been all night — flirting at the pub I'll bet.'

Jess watched, wide-eyed. She noticed Olivia crouched at the top of the stairs, biting nervously on her nightgown. She had not seen Jess. Down below, the feud raged on.

'Yeah, that would be just what you'd think wouldn't it. Typical woman — can't wait to accuse a man of—'

'—John why are you doing this to me?'

'To *you*? That's a laugh.'

'I'm not laughing John.'

'I don't see what it has to do with you, I'm not affecting you.'

Margi's voice quivered as it lowered. 'Surely, it's not too much to ask for you to come home at a sensible time occasionally … have a normal meal with us, take an interest in your daughter?'

'Damn you woman. I've had enough of this!' He pointed

his finger fiercely in her face. Margi was sobbing loudly and uncontrollably now, as her husband headed for the stairs.

'Next time don't bother coming home!' she screamed after him, slumping into a heap on the floor, her hands over her face.

Olivia was the first to move as her father made his way up the stairs. She disappeared inside her bedroom. Jess waited until the last second before she backed into her room. She watched the outraged figure storm past. The strong smell of liquor and work clothes wafted after him. He did not seem to see Jess at all. When the bathroom door had been slammed shut and the resulting rattle throughout the house had died down, Jess moved out into the hall again, just far enough to see Margi leaning limply against the side of an arm chair near where she'd collapsed. Her legs were folded beneath her and her head was bowed low. Olivia's face appeared again from behind her door and watched her mother through the banisters. Jess looked at her, watching her mother's distress.

'Don't just stand there, do something!' hissed Jess before turning back to her room and slamming her own door with equal force and feeling to that which John had used. Jess pounded her fists a couple times against the pillow before falling onto it heavily, deflated. Her whole body shook with anger. It wasn't fair. *It just wasn't fair!*

Jess had been giving Olivia cold looks ever since they'd been together in the kitchen that morning. She popped her toast out of the toaster and tossed it onto a plate. Margi stood by the sink, cutting sandwiches and talking of some up-coming charity event she was involved in. Olivia was pouring dog food into a bowl. Jess felt the urge to comment on the appropriate breakfast Olivia was preparing herself but decided against it because Margi was in the room.

The kitchen fell completely silent when John entered a moment later. Jess could feel his footsteps sending shock waves through the wooden floor. For the first time she was able to get a proper look at him. His hair was ragged. It fell in light brown tufts almost to his shoulders. He was unshaven. The prickly bronze-red stubble on his face seemed to warn her away. His face looked moody, and Jess thought she recognised impatience in his eyes. The rusty coloured eyebrows were bushy and almost joined in the middle. His face was round and large, tempting anyone to mess with him. His shoulders were broad and carried quite an amount of meat on them — and Jess figured, their fair share of fat. He wore work clothes, like those he had on the night before.

'Morning,' he muttered. Jess thought he looked guilty.

'Morning dear,' Margi chirped.

'Good morning Dad,' Olivia said over her shoulder, as she floated out the back door with the bowl of dog food. Jess couldn't believe it. They were acting as if nothing had happened. *Had they forgiven him?* she thought in horror.

'You must be Jess,' John said to her, reaching out his hand.

She looked at him in surprise. 'Yes — yes I am.' After a moment's hesitation she took his hand, feeling strange — like she was condoning a murderer. He squeezed her hand warmly and smiled a crooked smile. She looked up into his face. John withdrew his hand and gave her a light pat on the shoulder. Then without saying any more, he turned his back to her and began rummaging through the cereal boxes in the cupboard. Jess began buttering her cold toast. The butter clung thickly to it, refusing to melt.

Olivia came back into the kitchen. 'I'm going now,' she chimed.

'Yes, bye dear, have a nice day,' her mother replied.

'See you love,' John said, without looking up from the oat flakes that he was pouring into a bowl.

Jess was glad to see Olivia go off to school. After demolishing the last of her gluggy toast, Jess drifted into the living room. She noticed a pillow and several blankets strewn untidily over the couch, which looked as though it had been slept on the night before. Jess heard John call out that he was going to work, then the screen door banged. She wandered back into the kitchen.

'Can I go out?' she asked.

'Where are you going?'

'Just for a walk.'

'Of course you can, you're not a prisoner here.'

Jess hesitated. Was this a reference to her past? She wasn't sure.

Margi continued. 'You're free to come and go,' she said from behind the open fridge door. This idea appealed to Jess, although she might have taken it more literally than it was meant. She strolled out the back door, over the lawn, past the neat rows of rose bushes, and out of the yard, into the streets of the unfamiliar town.

Olivia bustled through the front door and threw her school bag onto the floor. Margi, who was late for a hair appointment, flew past her.

'Hi darling,' she said hurriedly as she disappeared out the door and down the front steps.

'*Hi darling,*' Jess, who was reclined on the couch, mimicked smugly.

Olivia gave her a look that told her she was clearly not impressed with the way Jess appeared so comfortable and relaxed. Standing in front of her with her hands on her hips she said, 'You're really making yourself at home, aren't you?'

'Why not, this *is* my home now.'

'Think again, Miss,' Olivia muttered.

'Excuse me, but your parents wanted me to be part of your family,' said Jess, defending herself.

'Parent. *Singular*. Dad didn't want you either.'

'Then why am I here?' Jess's voice became aggravated.

'One of Mum's little stunts, I guess. She's a fool, I say. Doesn't know what you street bums are like. Lucky I do though.'

'How dare you make judgement about something you know nothing about. Just because you've had everything in your life handed to you on a golden platter makes you think you're the queen of the earth? Well let me tell you something you stuck up little tart — you're *not!*' Jess spoke quickly and abrasively. 'I don't know what your problem is, but I can tell you that a good kick up the arse would fix it. You think that anyone whose parents are dead or whose dad beats them up is a social outcast.' Jess paused to catch her breath while Olivia's expression turned icy cold.

'That's not what I meant, I didn't say anything about your dad,' she said.

'Well what did you mean then?' Jess challenged, her voice still raised.

'You had to come here and invade our lives, didn't you?' Olivia spat accusingly. Her face was flushed pink and tears appeared in the corners of her eyes.

'I've barely been here two days.'

'And I've been here sixteen years, so I think that makes it a bit more my home than yours, don't you?'

'Fine, have your stupid home. I don't need it. It's not as though I exactly asked to come here. I don't need charity from you or your stupid parents. I'd probably be better off on the streets,' Jess said, wishing to have nothing more to say to her.

'Don't let me stop you,' Olivia snapped hastily.

Until now, Jess had remained on the couch. She leapt to her feet, and in a second she was only centimetres away from Olivia's face, barely managing to keep her fists by her sides.

'Why don't you go and find someone else to bitch off at, I'm not interested!' She turned away, but Olivia hadn't finished.

'We were happy before you came here.'

Jess turned suddenly to face her again. 'Oh yeah, sure. What happened last night — you call that *happy* do you?'

'Just stay away from me *Jess*.' She stated Jess's name in a mocking tone.

'With pleasure your majesty,' Jess retorted airily, and left the room, leaving Olivia standing in the middle of the room wiping away her tears.

Jess went outside and down to the bottom of the yard. She slammed her fists against the rattly corrugated iron fence. When she'd finished, she tossed her hair out of her face, took a deep breath and glanced down at the blood seeping from her grazed knuckles. It was then that she saw an elderly lady with a pair of garden secateurs in her hand, peering at her over the neighbour's fence with a horrified look on her face.

Ignoring her, Jess looked back at the fence that she'd let out her anger upon. She had a feeling that before too many weeks had passed, that fence would have taken quite a beating.

CHAPTER 6

Zac was in hospital for two weeks. Apart from the surface wounds, Jess had given him a bad dose of concussion and some bruising to the skull. They'd kept him in for observation until the swelling had gone down, which was apparently a potentially life-threatening complication. Jess had found all this out via the police. They'd also found out more about him. It wasn't his first offence and he didn't try to deny much of it.

'You mean he confessed?' Jess had asked.

'Not in so many words, but it makes the whole business a lot easier,' Constable West had told her. He'd come to see her himself, having taken a special interest in the case. Jess had tried to imagine Zac lying in a hospital bed, his bullet still around his neck. She'd shuddered.

'Won't I have to go to court?' she'd asked.

'Not necessarily, but we'll let you know of any developments in that regard. You must be relieved?'

Relieved? Jess didn't know what she felt. It was a strange mixture of feelings, all swimming together in a giant pool. She'd suddenly felt removed from the whole situation. It had happened just over two weeks ago, but now seemed like it had been in another life. She'd tried hard to forget that night.

'Yeah — relieved,' she repeated, sounding vacant. So much had been happening lately that she'd managed not to think too much about what would happen when they finally interrogated Zac. She was just glad that she probably wouldn't have to face him, not even in some courtroom. She didn't care what happened to him now, but only hoped that she'd never have to see him again.

Each morning, John would walk through the house whistling and being generally cheerful to everyone, including Jess, who thought he was doing pretty well for someone who didn't want her around. The disturbance of the first night seemed to have blown over and hadn't recurred. In the evenings, however, John was listless and tired. His mood swings were unpredictable, especially if he'd had a drink or two, but he stayed away from Jess at these times.

Most mornings, the couch seemed to have been slept on. There was apparently still some residue left from that conflict — or perhaps a different one, Jess wondered. Margi seemed to take it all in her stride, and nothing was ever said about it. Jess often felt like an intruder in their private feud and as if their conversations were censored for her benefit, or perhaps for their own. Maybe that was why she was there. It had been puzzling her why a family with something to hide would want her there at all. Margi's reply in the sitting room that first day had not entirely satisfied her. Perhaps in her ignorance Jess was supposed to be acting as a kind of silent referee. Did Margi think that bringing a stranger into the house would suppress whatever it was that was going on? Whatever their motives, she knew there was no place in this family for her.

During one of John's better moods, the family was seated in the living room, eating dinner in front of the television. Olivia was stretched out gracefully on the rug, with her plate of food perched on her stomach. It seemed like she spent most of her time making sure she looked perfect or talking on the phone. Jess sat cross-legged on the floor, not far from Olivia. She could smell her perfume, which was sickeningly strong. Jess had become bored with the television show. She was observing Olivia critically. She compared the clothes Olivia wore to her own. Jess was sure she hadn't seen her wearing the same outfit twice. All of Olivia's clothes were of the latest season's fashion. Jess wore denim jeans and a plain T-shirt that Margi had bought for her several days after she'd arrived. The only garments that she owned were the old shabby ones she'd been wearing for months. She had refused to wear the refuge clothes at Wellingwood. She didn't like the idea of wearing clothes that had adorned someone else's body.

For a while Jess watched Olivia eating her meal. Perhaps she was trying to find faults with everything she did. As her gaze drifted she noticed what looked like a large purple bruise on her tanned right thigh, partly covered by her short white skirt. Out of the corner of her eye, Olivia noticed her gaze. Quickly she pulled her skirt down to hide it. Her face looked pink and uncomfortable. She placed her plate on the floor. She seemed to have suddenly lost her appetite. Jess's eyes lingered on Olivia's face for several moments, then she turned away, and continued to pick at her salad.

'So Jess, how about we get you enrolled at school

tomorrow?' John said suddenly. It was obvious that he had become disinterested in the TV program as well.

'I don't want to go to school,' Jess replied quickly, without looking up from her meal.

'Oh come on, what are you going to do with yourself otherwise?' he questioned, without a hint of annoyance in his voice.

'I'll find something,' she said in an equally neutral tone.

'Like what?'

'Anything.'

'Nothing illegal I hope?' he said jovially. Jess didn't share his mood and shot him a sideways glance.

'She's going to grow marijuana under her bed.' No one took any notice of Olivia's comment, but she didn't seem to mind.

'School is a waste of time,' Jess said.

'I'm sorry, but the bottom line is that it's the law to go to school at least until you're fifteen,' John told her patiently, clearly deciding it was time to take the direct approach.

'Stuff the law. I'm sick of the law.'

John read into this. 'It's been tough for you lately I guess.'

Jess wished everyone would stop trying to be so supportive and understanding. It annoyed her intensely. Everything did. She ignored him. Suddenly something on the TV grabbed his interest again and the conversation fizzled out.

Margi worked Mondays and Fridays, waitressing at a local cafe. She was gone by the time Jess got up in the mornings and didn't return until at least six in the evening. She was usually too tired to cook after work on those days, so it was left up to John, Olivia and Jess to get themselves something to eat if they were hungry. Jess enjoyed this independence and didn't even give a thought to the strain on Margi's face at night.

Margi always waited until everyone else had gone to bed before she curled up on the couch with her pillow and blankets. Jess once said to her, 'It can't be very comfortable?'

'What?'

'Sleeping on the couch.'

Margi had given her a resentful glare, warning her away from the subject.

Jess still felt like an outsider, removed from the lives of the people around her. At the same time, she was glad she was not the centre of *this* family feud.

It was now Monday afternoon. The day was sunny and invited Jess to explore it. She had left the house at eleven and wandered through the town. She went past the lonely looking houses, to the cemetery by the plantation forest. She found graves the most fascinating things. She then walked through the forest and beyond. Jess had always loved to roam. It allowed her to forget things.

It was now four o'clock as she walked back up the driveway. She entered the house through the back door. As she walked through the kitchen she heard voices coming from upstairs. The door to the passage was closed. Listening like she had the first night she'd been there, she tried to identify the owners of the voices. She opened the door and poked her head through.

'Dad, please!' She heard Olivia's voice plead. What was John doing home so early? Jess walked along the hall to the bottom of the staircase.

'Kid, you really need to be taught a lesson.'

'No—Dad!' Jess could hear Olivia sobbing loudly. 'No, please, not this time.' She was whimpering, sounding desperate and afraid. Jess knew that sound well. At Wellingwood there had been many disturbed voices, crying through the night — all night. It sounded the same.

She began to climb the stairs, slowly, trying not to make any noise. The voices grew louder as she reached the top. There was a light on in the study, and in Olivia's bedroom, where the noise was coming from. The door was almost shut, but still the sound reached Jess clearly. She crept up to the door, her heart beating rapidly.

Through the tiny gap between the door frame and the door where it was hinged, she saw Olivia on the bed, and John, standing over her. For a moment her vision was blocked by his movement in front of her, then she heard the all too familiar thump, and the subsequent squeal of pain. John moved to the other side of the bed and Jess could see things clearly again — the raised arm, the girl cowering on the bed, shielding her face with both hands.

'You stupid girl, why do you force me to do this to you?' John growled.

'I didn't mean what I said!' Olivia cried frantically.

'Yeah, I'll bet. I'll teach you to be disrespectful.'

Jess was frozen. She couldn't watch any longer. Even though she didn't like Olivia, the scene was all too vivid. Visions of her own father flashed before her, as real as if it were happening at that moment. The sound effects were no illusion, though. She stood motionless for a minute or two, grasping onto the stairs rail.

When John came out of the room, Jess was tucked out of sight in the bathroom. She waited until he had clumped heavily down the stairs, and she'd heard the outside door slam, before crossing the hall to peer into Olivia's bedroom. She was sitting hunched up on the floor, between her bed and the wall. Her face was wet with tears and her eyes were red and puffy. Jess couldn't imagine this being the smooth, cocky, full-of-herself young lady that she saw every day. Jess walked a little further into the room. Olivia did not try to evict her, as perhaps she normally would have, but sat there in silence.

'Tell me why, Olivia,' Jess demanded. Olivia waited a moment before answering.

'I was rude to him.'

'That doesn't give him the right—' Jess stopped herself. She stood looking down at her.

'It's been worse since you've been here.'

Jess wondered whether she was supposed to feel guilty. She didn't.

'Does he come home just to beat you up?'

'He says he comes home to check on me, see that I'm all

right while Mum's away. He'll sometimes lay into me, if he can find a reason. Today was bad.'

'Does Margi know?'

Olivia shook her head.

'Why do you let him do it?'

'I have no choice, I can't burden Mum. She's got enough to worry about.' Her tongue regained its knife.

'Personally I wouldn't stand for it anymore.'

'I deserved it.'

Jess folded her arms and scratched her face. Olivia broke into a new spasm of sobs.

'He tells you that I guess?' Jess said.

'What about your dad?' Olivia asked, looking up at her now.

'Huh. What about him?'

'He used to hit you, didn't he?'

'Yeah.'

'What did you do?'

'I told him where to go.'

Olivia shook her head. 'I couldn't, it'd just make him worse.'

'Mmm, it does.'

Olivia let her head fall against the bed. She stared at the floor. Her tears dripped from her chin and sank into the pile of the carpet. After a short, still silence, she began to speak again, weaving between the spasmodic gasps of her crying.

'He never used to hit me. He was just like a dream father — loving and kind.' This recollection made the tears flow faster. 'About a year ago his drinking got worse, and he didn't seem to love Mum and me anymore. But I just can't understand it, he never lays a finger on her.' Olivia spoke slowly and painfully. 'Perhaps he knows she's stronger than me.' She allowed herself a tiny smile.

'Then why does she sleep on the couch? How do you know he doesn't touch her?' Jess queried.

'I just know, okay.' Olivia tried to shout her words, but they came out emotion-charged and wavering.

'Why don't you tell someone?' Jess continued, standing her ground.

'I can't, he's still my father,' said Olivia.

'Some father,' Jess muttered.

'Don't you dare tell anyone about this,' Olivia warned.

'It's got nothing to do with me.' Jess turned her back on Olivia and left the room.

Jess made a resolution never to trust John after that, not that she had anyway. Whenever she looked at his face she saw her own father, and she didn't like it.

Jess was in the living room, paging through the newspaper when he came through the front door that evening. He looked different to her, although she knew he wasn't. He greeted her as he passed. Jess didn't reply. She wasn't angry with him because she felt sorry for Olivia, but because she knew what kind of a person he really was. She was glad that she knew though and wondered how many other secrets were being kept from her. Before going through to the kitchen, John glanced at Jess. He must have decided that she was too absorbed in the paper to answer his greeting. Jess's eyes ran across the headings on the page before her: *Rape Victim Tells All; Domestic Violence Erupts in Eastern Suburbs; Man Charged over Wife's Murder; Self Defence — At What Cost?* She threw the paper onto the floor. It landed in a deranged heap. She got up and left the house, feeling summoned once more to roam the streets.

When she returned it was late. The street lights were on and there was a dim glow from behind the curtains in the houses along the street. Jess found John and Olivia at the dining table, demolishing large helpings of ice cream and caramel topping. Jess's stomach growled.

'Where have you been?' John asked.

'Nowhere.'

'Is it a nice place?' John asked.

'What?' Jess screwed up her face.

'Nowhere. You go there a lot, don't you?'

Jess was not in the mood for humour, especially from John. She ignored him and walked into the kitchen to get something to eat.

'There're some sausages in the fridge if you want them,' John called after her.

'Thanks.' Suddenly Jess felt like becoming a vegetarian.

When they thought she had gone, John spoke softly to Olivia. 'Why is she so cold?'

'I don't know, maybe she resents us.'

Jess, who was still just on the other side of the door, heard every word they said.

'But we've given her a home, haven't we?' John continued, puzzled.

'Perhaps that's what she resents,' Olivia suggested.

John paused, trying to work out exactly what she meant. He swallowed his mouthful. 'Do you know something that I don't?'

Instead of responding with a smart reply, as Jess probably would have, she meekly said, 'No ...'

Jess walked back into the room carrying a plate containing a single sausage and a slice of bread. As she sat down, Margi came into the dining room and deposited her bag on a chair. She had returned home weary and jaded looking as usual. Jess thought that the freshest she'd seen her was the day she'd arrived. She seemed to be going downhill. Margi sat down opposite Jess.

'Can I get you something to eat, Mum?' Olivia asked.

'No it's okay, I had something at the cafe,' Margi replied without looking at her daughter. After John and Olivia had left the table, Margi, who had appeared to be thinking deeply, said, 'I've been thinking about this school thing.'

Jess's heart sank.

'I think we'll wait until after the holidays to enrol you. They're only a week away, so there wouldn't be much point in doing it before then,' Margi said.

'No, there wouldn't.' Jess said. There was a pause. 'I don't really need to go to school, do I?' Jess tried one last time.

'You know the answer to that,' Margi replied, getting up from the table with Jess's empty plate. Jess was left alone. She didn't know what she would do if she didn't go to school, but she didn't want to go.

She felt helpless. She had agreed to come here hoping that somehow it would be the start of a new life. She didn't seem to be gaining any ground though. Something was preventing her, she didn't know what. She was confused. What was she supposed to do? These days the only time she felt almost completely at ease was when she wandered aimlessly through the town, the woods and the graveyard — alone. Jess realised though that living on the streets was not the answer. But there were no other options.

On Friday night Olivia invited some friends over. They were from her school, where Jess would soon be going. It was a public school, half a kilometre from their home. Jess had often walked past it and looked in through the metal gates that were like those at the entrance to the cemetery, only not as fancy, nor as rusty. She thought it looked too much like Wellingwood, although in reality the resemblance was slight.

Olivia's friends came in dribs and drabs. Jess answered a knock at the door and found herself face to face with a boy about Olivia's age. He had dark hair that fell to one side, held together with a large amount of styling product. He was chewing gum and carried a bag over one shoulder. He looked for a moment at Jess, then stepped casually through the door, with a slight grin on his face.

'Livi didn't tell me we were having such good-looking company tonight.' He spoke as he chewed. His voice was a little scratchy.

'I live here,' Jess said, feeling uncomfortable. She stood by the door, looking into his face. The boy stayed still, watching her also. 'Um, Olivia's upstairs,' Jess finally said, trying to sound businesslike, but failing miserably.

'Thanks,' he said, lifting his eyebrows and walking

towards the stairs with his thumbs in his pockets. Jess pushed the front door closed. She didn't like his manner at all.

As he entered Olivia's bedroom, he greeted the three girls and other boy who were already sitting on the floor amongst piles of magazines and food.

'Hi, Travis,' one of the girls sang out. Travis dumped his bag on the floor and spoke to Olivia.

'Hey, who's the babe downstairs?'

Olivia almost choked on a corn chip she'd been eating. 'That's nobody. She's not part of our party tonight.'

'Why?' said the girl who had spoken to Travis.

'Because she's a loser.'

'She seemed okay to me,' the girl argued.

'She's only fourteen, Renee,' Olivia added, screwing up her nose.

'Who cares, as long as she's—' Travis stopped mid-sentence, leaving the rest up to the imaginations of the others.

'I bet she feels left out,' Renee pitied.

'Yeah, why don't you invite her in?' Travis said.

'That'll be the day when I ever invite her to do anything.'

'Then I'll do it,' Travis said.

'What is it with you guys anyway?' said Olivia.

'You know the saying, the more the merrier,' Travis replied.

'Yes exactly,' the third girl said with a grin.

'C'mon.'

'No.'

'Olivia don't be a spoil sport.'

'I give up, let her in. I can see I'm not going to get any peace until you do.' Olivia knew she was out-numbered. 'You'll never be able to get her in here anyway,' she added.

Travis found Jess in the kitchen.

'Hi,' he said.

'What do *you* want?'

'Nothing, I just came to talk to you. Is that all right?'

'I don't know. It depends.'

Travis obviously took this as a yes. 'So how are you going?' he continued.

'I'll live.' Jess stood in front of him with her hands behind her back. Travis was leaning casually against the fridge, blocking her way should she want to leave the room.

'You don't like me much do you?' Travis said.

'Should I?'

'Yeah, I'm a real nice guy,' he said, grinning down at her.

'You know what I think? I think you've got a serious ego problem.' Jess said. Travis seemed to take this as a compliment.

'Thanks,' he said, flicking his hair out of his face with an exaggerated upward toss of his head. Jess was too disgusted to speak. 'So, what are you doing?' Travis went on.

'Nothing just at the moment.' Jess was irritated by his smoothness. She shifted restlessly on the spot, still glaring at him.

'Why don't you join us upstairs?'

'I don't think Olivia would be too happy about that somehow.'

'Nah, she's cool about it,' Travis assured her.

'Yeah, and pigs fly too,' Jess replied, sensing that this was a trap.

'Is that a yes or a no?'

As he stood in the doorway looking down at her, she decided that he was good looking.

'I've got better things to do than spend my evening with a bunch of stuck-up sixteen-year-olds thank you very much.'

'C'mon … don't be shy,' he pleaded.

'I am not shy!' she said fiercely, growing increasingly more annoyed by his persistence.

'Scared of me are you then?'

'You are so full of yourself.'

'So they tell me,' Travis answered cockily. Jess had had enough. She tried to push past him, but he was bigger and stronger than her. He gripped her arm.

'C'mon Jess what have you got to lose?'

'All right!' she yelled. 'Just get your hands off me.'

When he heard this, Travis let her go.

'Fantastic. You'll have a great time I know,' he said with a smile, and headed up the stairs looking pleased with himself. Jess followed him, telling herself that she was only going to prove to him that she was not the things he had said she was.

'I'm Travis by the way,' Travis said to her as they reached the landing.

'Oh, right.' Jess said disinterestedly.

When Travis opened the bedroom door all four faces turned to look at them, or rather, to look at Jess, who didn't smile, but looked around the room at the others and the mess they'd already created.

'Hi Jess,' chirped one of the girls after she'd finished her mouthful of popcorn.

'Hi,' the rest of the group chorused, except for Olivia, who simply rolled her eyes.

Jess tried to make out what they were thinking of her as Travis closed the door and joined the group. 'Hello,' she said uncomfortably. A girl with wavy blonde hair smiled at her warmly.

'Have a seat,' she said, gesturing towards the floor. Jess sat.

'Let's put some music on,' said the other boy, who was sitting next to Olivia.

'Good idea. What kind of music do you like Jess?' the blonde girl asked her.

'I don't know, anything,' she replied quickly, glancing around to see who was looking at her, and finding every face turned curiously in her direction.

'Okay, I'll choose something then,' the girl said, scrolling through a play list. As she did so, Travis sat down next to Jess. He smelt of cheap aftershave.

Olivia was shuffling a pack of cards. 'Do you want to play, Jess?' she asked in a sugar-sweet voice.

'What are you playing?' Jess inquired.

'How does strip poker grab you?' Travis said with a grin. *Great,* Jess thought, *just what I need, first a smooth-talking male with his hormones out of control, and now strip poker.*

'Sure, I'll play,' she said, still expressionless. As Olivia dealt the cards, Jess studied each of her friends individually. The blonde girl seemed lively and friendly. Her round face was bright and alert. She had a small turned up nose and rich brown eyes. Her hair was short and a light yellowy blonde. She had obviously had highlights put in. She sat cross-legged.

Next to her was another girl, probably slightly taller, and more sedate looking. She had light orange shoulder-length hair. Jess wondered whether it was her natural colour. It was all the same length and hung loosely. She was pretty and delicate. She wore almost as much jewellery as Olivia, who sat next to her. Olivia's hair was in a single French braid that hung over her shoulder. Her earrings were fancy, and her long fingernails painted bright red. She wore a ring on every finger.

Apart from Travis, the only other boy in the room sat on Olivia's other side. He had blonde hair, styled with almost as much artificial adhesive as Travis's. He looked to be a laidback, easy going sort of guy. He had a pointed chin and dashing blue eyes. Everyone was wearing stylish, new-looking clothes. They all appeared very mature. Jess thought they looked like they were going to a fashion show, not gathering at a friend's house. She felt out of place in her plain clothes and lack of accessories.

Olivia had finished dealing and they started to play. Travis moved closer to Jess. She had not seemed to notice, so he leaned in a bit further. Jess had noticed. She shifted in the opposite direction, giving him a dirty look. The game continued. Every time Olivia lost she took off one of her rings.

'That's cheating!' the blonde girl protested.

'No it's not, it's being resourceful,' Olivia answered. Soon there was a large pile of jewellery in the middle of the circle. When Travis lost a game, he asked Jess to take his shirt off for him. She declined the offer coldly. Travis only laughed. Jess had not lost a round yet.

The time ticked by. The game continued. The blonde girl lost the next game. Everyone watched her grow bright pink.

'What's the matter? Not much left to take off, eh, Layla?' Travis laughed. The only piece of clothing that remained on her body was her skimpy yellow dress. Her underwear had already been skilfully extracted. All of them watched, waiting to see what she would do. After a moment or two, Layla stood up, revealing tanned slender legs. 'Excuse me, I have to go to the toilet,' she said in a shaky voice. In a second she had disappeared from the room. Jess sat there, stunned by how seriously they were taking the game.

'Oooh, she's going shy on us,' the blonde boy said with a laugh.

'I'm sure you would too if you had to take all your clothes off in front of us, Josh,' said the orange-haired girl, whom Jess had heard someone call Renee. He grinned.

'I don't know about that,' he said, partially getting up from his reclined position. He put an arm around Olivia, who had been unusually quiet that evening, and kissed her on the cheek. 'I know Livi wouldn't mind, would you?' Josh's affection sparked something in Travis, and he slipped an arm around Jess's shoulders. She squirmed uncomfortably but didn't make any move to throw it off.

'Let's keep playing, don't worry about Layla,' Olivia said, dealing the cards once again. They played their hands.

'You lose, Jess,' Josh smiled. She felt herself turning red, the way Layla had.

'C'mon, you haven't lost before this,' Renee urged. Jess looked around. Once again she felt them all watching her. She didn't move or say a word. They waited to see what she was going to do. Travis, who had taken Jess's acceptance of his affection so far as a sign of encouragement, gave her a devilish smile. He drew her close to him, so that her face was just centimetres away from his. She could feel his hot breath on her cheek. Suddenly something inside Jess snapped. She tore away from his grasp and leapt to her feet. Travis looked up at her, startled. Everyone's eyes followed her. Jess flung the door open and ran out, past Layla who stood in the hall, and down the stairs. She dashed through the living room, jumped over the sofa where Margi's pillow and blanket lay, and burst through the front door, not pausing until she stood on the nature strip outside.

I've got to get away, she thought, *away from them.* She began to jog slowly down the darkened street. The sound of her feet on the asphalt echoed loudly off the buildings. She remembered the look on their faces just before she fled the room, and shuddered. She punished herself as she ran — *I should have known. They're Olivia's friends. I should have known ...*

Jess reached the cemetery, breathing heavily as she walked through the high wrought iron gates. She had never been in a graveyard at night before. It looked so different in the dark. She walked tentatively between the headstones, which cast dark shadows on the ground and over the other graves. The shadows moved as she moved. Crickets chirped from their hiding places in the grass.

Jess came to the row of tall pine trees on the edge of the forest. She looked up at the starry sky and slowly backed up to lean against a tree. She gasped when the tree moved out from behind her as she eased against it. Spinning around she saw that her tree was a man — an old man in a large brown overcoat. Jess jumped back in fright and was about to run back towards the gates when he spoke.

'I'm sorry, I didn't mean to startle you,' he said in a deep European accent. She paused, there was nothing threatening in his voice. She swallowed and let out her breath but stepped back so that she was a safe distance from him. She was still out of breath from her run. The man stood still for a moment, staring past the trees as if he had forgotten she was there. Then he looked around.

'It's beautiful here at this time of night, isn't it?' he said.

'Yeah, I guess,' Jess agreed cautiously.

'So, are you coming or going?' he asked her. There was silence for a moment.

'A bit of both I guess,' Jess answered vaguely, her mind still vividly on that evening.

'Ah, like that, is it?' The man nodded knowingly. 'I come here when I have a problem. It helps me to think more clearly.' He looked at her over the high collar of his coat. Jess could only slightly make out the features of his face, though she could tell he had high cheek bones. The moonlight occasionally fell across his face, allowing her a glimpse of the dark deep-set eyes. She knew he had a beard from the shape of his face silhouetted against the line of trees. She could not tell if he was fat or thin because he was covered almost from head to toe by the overcoat.

'Call me Jack,' he said, reaching out his hand. After a moment Jess took it, not knowing what she should make of him, but something kept her there. 'What's your name?'

Jess hesitated.

'Or don't you have one?'

'Sometimes I feel like I don't have one,' she replied existentially.

'A few hassles at home, eh?'

'Something like that.'

There was a long pause, then Jack spoke again. 'It's funny how the cares of the world seem so tiny and insignificant when you're out here isn't it?'

Jess nodded her head slowly. She knew what he meant. Despite the churning of her stomach and being wary of this stranger, she felt strangely at peace.

'Do you come here a lot?' Jess asked him.

'When I feel the need to let my mind go free. The hard part though, is catching it again. People say I'm losing my mind, but you know, I've never lost it once.'

'Maybe that's my problem — I'm losing my mind, I'm going insane ...' Jess tapered off her sentence. She fully believed it at that moment.

'I couldn't say, I don't know you. Ask someone who cares, they'll tell you if you are or not.'

'But nobody cares.' Jess choked on her words.

'I know how you feel. Some of the poor old buggers here probably felt the same way.' He gestured to the graves around them. 'It's strange, you know, it feels like these guys are my friends, even though I never knew them.'

'It seems as though you have to be dead before you're appreciated,' Jess said. They both stood gazing out into the night in silence. 'I think I'll stay here till morning.' Jess spoke softly, almost in a whisper.

'I'd love to stay, but I really must be getting back. Not that anyone will miss me.' Jack turned to leave. 'Thanks for the chat.' Jess watched him walk away. His hunched-up figure grew smaller and more distant, and the sound of his feet crackling on the dry leaves died away as he made his way through the graveyard and into the trees beyond.

'No one will miss me either,' Jess said softly.

She suddenly realised how cold it was, and how lightly she was dressed. Shivering, she walked back toward the iron gates. There she sat down on a rusted park bench, which moved under her weight. She leaned her head back against the concrete pillar that held the gate on its hinges. She sighed and stared once more into the sky and the galaxies beyond. The world was motionless around her, and she was completely and utterly alone.

CHAPTER 8

'Jess, are you listening to me?'

Jess looked up from the television show she was watching. Margi stood looking down at her. 'I'm going shopping now okay, then I'm going to work. Do you need anything from the shop?'

'Not at the moment.'

'Next week I'll take you and Olivia into the city to shop. How would you like that? Tonight Olivia won't be home until after seven. She's got hockey practice, so it'll just be you and John here for dinner, all right?'

'Mmm,' Jess said disinterestedly.

'Oh, and I almost forgot, someone from the department is coming to see you this morning, to see how you're getting along.'

'Great.'

'You will cooperate, won't you?' Margi asked, almost impatiently.

'Mmm.'

Margi waited for a moment to see if what she'd said had sunk in, but no indication of this came. She left without saying any more.

It was the Monday morning after Olivia's party. After a while Jess became bored with the TV. She flicked it off but stayed where she was on the couch. She realised she must have been dozing when she was suddenly jolted by the sound of the doorbell. She made her way to the door, in no real hurry to reach it. When she did, she opened it to find her youth worker standing on the steps. She let the woman inside and led her through to the living room.

'I guess Margi told you I was coming.' she said.

'Yeah, she said you were coming to check up on me.'

'I wouldn't say to check up on you. I'm here to see how you've settled in, and to discuss any problems.'

Any problems? How could she discuss her problems with a stranger? But everyone was a stranger. The Pullins were virtual strangers although she had lived with them for weeks. She knew no one outside the family other than the youth worker.

'No, there's no problems,' Jess assured her.

'Can we sit down and have a talk?' The visitor smiled. Jess sat back down on the couch, thinking of how much she detested the way these people smiled at her, as if they understood.

'So how are you going? Tell me about what has happened.' She was sitting on the edge of the seat with her hands clasped around her knees. Her skirt protruded a few centimetres over her knees like a cliff on the edge of a mountain. She waited for Jess's response.

'Nothing's happened. I haven't been to school yet or anything.'

The youth worker looked surprised. 'Why ever not?'

'Margi says she's waiting till next term to enrol me since the holidays are so close.'

'Oh I see. I thought you just had the day off. When can I talk to Margi? Is she home?'

'No, she's at work, I'm the only one here.'

Over the following hour the woman asked Jess questions about the family, and what she thought about various things — all quite unnecessary Jess thought. She tried to answer them all in a way that no more interrogation could be squeezed from her answers. When the discussion was over, Jess let her guest out the front door and wandered back into the living room. She sank into an armchair and looked around the quiet room. She watched the clock on the mantel piece as it ticked. The ticking seemed loud in the silence of the empty house.

'Now what?' Jess said out loud. Was it a question about the rest of the day or the rest of her life? She didn't know.

'I'm going to go crazy if I sit here in this house much longer. I think I must be losing my mind like Jack said, I'm talking to myself.' With a sigh she got up and went outside. 'Maybe the mailman's been,' she said, even though she knew there would be nothing for her.

Walking down the gravel drive Jess could feel the stones prickling through her socks, which was all she wore on her feet. She looked into the mailbox. It was empty. She slammed down the lid of the box and made her way back into the house. Jess paced through the rooms. She walked into Olivia's room.

She looked at the things on the dresser, and then in the dresser drawers. They were full of socks and bras and little folded bits of paper. She moved over to the window.

She had not spoken to Olivia since Friday night when they had played strip poker. Jess resented her for what had happened and believed she had put Travis up to what he'd done, just to spite her. Now in the quiet bedroom she could almost hear Olivia's laughter echoing around her. She was angry at herself for having gone along with them. She was determined never to get involved with anything of Olivia's again. Now was the perfect opportunity to get her revenge. She looked over at the highly ornamented dressing table. Her eyes rested on an elaborate china figure. She pictured it falling to the floor, smashing into thousands of pieces. It would be an accident. *Olivia should never have left the window open, so the wind could catch it.* Jess looked at it for several moments then turned away and walked out of the room. It was a stupid thing to even consider. She was letting Olivia get to her. She would not do that — would not stoop to her level.

That afternoon Jess decided to do her laundry, for she was still searching for something to do. As she reached into the washing machine to pull out a shirt, she heard the sound of the front door opening. Jess straightened up and listened. She remembered hearing the mantel clock strike five a few minutes earlier. She thought it must be John. Reaching into the washing machine she pulled out a T-shirt and dropped it into the laundry basket. As she did so, she heard someone calling her name. It was John. His voice sounded strange and high. Jess left the laundry and went through to the living room. John was standing there. His eyes were half closed, and he was clutching the back of the couch for support. Jess drew in her breath. She stood there watching him.

'Jess,' he repeated.

'What?'

'Now is that a very respectful way to answer?' The tone of his voice seemed to wobble up and down. He had never reprimanded her for the way she spoke to him before. Jess did not know what to say to this. John moved a little closer to her. Now she could detect the smell of alcohol that flooded across the room. She stood clutching the back of a chair herself.

'What do you know about the state of my back fence?' he said.

'I don't know about the fence, but I know what state you're in,' Jess said bluntly. John's eyes widened.

'The fence!' he hollered, with volume Jess had never heard from him before. He looked angry.

'What about the stupid thing?' Jess was fast growing impatient with him.

'Listen here, young lady—' he began, but Jess interrupted.

'Why don't you leave me alone, and come back when you're sober,' she ventured warily.

This was too much for him to take. His anger boiled over. 'You little brat, I'll teach you.'

He'll teach me, hey? Jess thought. What was he going to do? She thought maybe he would lock her in her room, or she'd be made to skip dinner, but she was not prepared for what followed.

He advanced on her slowly. She had never been afraid of John before, but now she felt a pang of fear. Almost before she'd seen him raise his arm, she felt a stinging pain on the side of her face and the room went black for a moment. She put a hand to her face. When he saw that she wasn't going to move, he took another swing at her face. This time the blow hit her squarely on the cheek bone. Jess's head lurched back and hit the wall. She regained her balance and stared, wild-eyed into his face. The shock of what had just happened paralysed her. She didn't have any time to think. She felt something hit her in the stomach. Her body could not recoil for it was now rammed firmly against the wall. Winded, she doubled over, clutching her stomach and gasping to fill her lungs with air.

When she looked up, she saw him grasping in his raised hand a heavy brass replica of Ned Kelly, that had been standing on the bookshelf. She could see the veins in the whites of his eyes. Jess cast a momentary look around the room for a way out. She would have to get past him. She let out a terrified shriek as the weapon came towards her. It didn't make contact because her reflexes were faster than his impaired movement. He made another attempt, this time missing by at least half a metre. As he staggered, Jess managed to slip past him, making a mad dash towards the front door. Her foot caught on Margi's Persian rug and she fell awkwardly. The corner of the coffee table dug into her leg. She cried out in pain. John was over her in a moment, gripping her arm.

'Do you really think I'd let you go that easily?' John's voice rasped. His crooked teeth showed. She squirmed under his grip and putrid smell. He yanked at her roughly.

'Olivia might let you get away with it, but there's no way I'm going to!'

'What did she say?' John demanded.

'Nothing, I've seen what you do to her. You're a crazy bastard. I *hate* you!' She struggled to free herself from his grasp. John shook her back and forth violently.

'Get your hands off me! Just get them *off* me!' Jess began to scream loudly, hoping frantically that someone would hear her. He dropped her to the ground.

'Shut up! Be quiet!'

Jess stopped screaming. She had gotten all her breath back now.

'Sit there and don't make a sound.' John pointed to a chair. Jess sat, watching the blood drip from the deep cut on her leg. It ran down and soaked into her sock. She gripped the leg with both hands. There was fire in her eyes. She couldn't remember ever feeling more anger. She had never really believed that one day he would do this to her. She had been foolish for thinking he would never touch her. There was no way she could stay there now, there was just no way.

'I need to go to the toilet,' Jess said, trying to control her voice.

'You're just going to try to get out of the house.' John read her thoughts perfectly.

'No, I *really* need to go,' she pleaded. John gave in.

'I guess you can't get far just going upstairs,' he said. He had underestimated her cunning.

Jess limped to the doorway. Her wound stung with every step. Slowly she climbed the stairs. She paused at the top to look down at John, who sat watching her with steely eyes. Jess turned around and kept going. She went into her room and straight over to the window. She knew she had to hurry, before he came looking for her. Sliding the window open she looked down to the ground.

Jess had a history of climbing out of windows. Even at home with her parents she would sometimes crawl through the window of her bedroom when her father locked her in. That was before she'd grown too big for the tiny gap in the wall.

There was no other window below Jess's, just a sheer brick wall. She would have to jump to the ground. This was more than she was willing to risk. There was a drain-pipe running down the wall outside. She thought about this for a moment, then remembered her escapade at Wellingwood and decided she didn't want to take the same chance again. Suddenly an idea struck her. She went out into the hall and hurried quietly along it. The toilet was at the end. She went in and closed the door. Once inside the tiny room her attention was on only one thing — the high frosted glass window. Jess knew there was a tall birch tree just outside. Standing on the seat, she pulled at the latches on the screen. The seat creaked loudly. The window was small, perhaps too small, but it was her only hope. She had the screen out. She dropped it and it hit the tiles with a vibrating ring. Jess grimaced at the noise. With all her might she tried to slide the window open. It hadn't been opened for a long time. It finally came. She scrambled up onto the cistern and moved around uncomfortably to find the right position to climb out. She felt cramped and awkward as she gripped the curtain rod and was beginning to panic.

Finally, she managed to squeeze out the window, feet first. She held the branches of the tree which seemed to have grown in just the right place for someone wanting to exit this way. *It'd be just my luck if he was waiting at the bottom of the tree,* she thought despairingly. He wasn't. She reached the ground safely and looked back up the wall, where the curtains flapped out of the window. Suddenly the Pullin's dog appeared and started to yap excitedly when it saw her. She swore, hoping it wouldn't attract John's attention.

Jess brushed the dog aside and went quickly down the side of the house, the side furthest from the living room. She felt tense and excited. Butterflies were fluttering around in her stomach. She slipped quietly through the gate. Coming out at the front of the house, she cast a glance over in the direction of the living room window. The outside blinds were still drawn. Jess stole down the street. Until now she had forgotten the cut on her leg. It began to hurt again. As she walked however, it wasn't her physical pain that dominated her thoughts.

Jess, now over the initial shock, realised just what John had done. He had beaten her, just like her father used to do. Were all men the same? *I never should have trusted them,* she thought, referring to the Pullins. She was angry at Margi.

Why didn't she stop him? Jess hated them. She hated them more with every step she took. She felt crazy, half delirious.

Suddenly she heard the loud blast of a car horn very close to her. She jumped, then backed out of the way of a car which had been reversing out of a driveway. The sky was growing dull and the aura of night began to creep across the town. Jess was heading toward the brightly lit main street.

As she passed shop windows, the mannequins seemed to stare at her. She felt like she was in a dream. The glaring lights made it seem unreal. She found a coffee shop that was open and went inside. Jess sat herself down at a small corner table. She picked up the menu and surveyed the fine print. It had been a long time since she'd seen anything like it. The only thing she had read in recent weeks was the occasional article in the local paper, during her long day time hours at the Pullins.

'Can I help you there, Miss?'

Jess looked up into the face of a cheerful, round-faced woman, who was holding a pad of paper and a pencil, poised ready to write. 'Would you like to order something?'

'No, I'm all right.'

'Pardon me for saying so, but you don't look all right,' the woman said curiously.

Jess realised how she must have looked. She reached up to touch her cheek where she'd been hit but stopped herself. She wondered whether a bruise showed on her face. 'No, I'm all right, really.'

'Got into a fight or something, did you?' She reached down to wipe the blood from Jess's leg with a paper serviette.

'Sort of,' Jess mumbled.

'Kids will be kids, I guess.' The woman turned back toward the counter.

Jess sat there, absently toying with a salt shaker. She didn't realise how long she'd been sitting there, until the waitress came over to her and said:

'I'm sorry but you'll have to leave. We're closing up now.'

'What's the time?' Jess asked.

'It's nine o'clock.'

Jess got up and began to walk steadily toward the door.

'Are you sure you're all right?' the waitress asked one more time, eyeing Jess with concern and clutching a tea towel in front of her plump, apron-covered stomach.

'Fine, honestly.'

The cafe door closed behind her. She stood aimlessly on the pavement outside. The street was almost deserted, but still the security lights glowed from behind the shop windows. Not really knowing what else to do, Jess retreated to a bus shelter, just like she'd done the night she'd escaped from Wellingwood. Had anything really changed since then?

CHAPTER 9

The brakes hissed and the bus pulled to a screeching halt. The door slid open and several people hurried down the steps carrying umbrellas and bags. Jess was suddenly jolted from her slumber. Quickly she sat up and tried to regain her complete consciousness. The bus swung out from the curb and the people hurried on their way, not giving the dazed, untidy looking girl sitting in the bus shelter a sideways glance.

Jess picked herself up and stood on the footpath. She looked around. The street was busy for early in the morning — unusually busy, Jess thought. Although she had to admit that she had never been out in this particular town so early on a Tuesday morning — or any morning for that matter. Although she wasn't really sure what the time was.

She had no money. She had nothing this time. Finally, she started to move along the street, in the opposite direction to the hustle and bustle. Jess had realised that being conspicuous was a suicidal move. She was painfully aware that had she played it a little more safely last time, she would never have had to live with the Pullins. Her head was full of regrets.

The rain fell in large, heavy drops, splashing back off the ground and soaking Jess's shoes. A gale was blowing up from the west, bringing with it dark storm clouds, turning the sunny afternoon grey. Jess fought against the wind, shielding her face from the sting of the fast-moving drops of water.

It was June and getting colder by the day. Frosts were beginning to form at night, which was a sure sign of a southern winter setting in. Jess still wore only light clothes and was trying to ignore the chilling discomfort that she felt. She could see a shed up ahead of her, probably a farm machinery shed. She began to run towards it. A barbed wire fence stood between her and the building. Several minutes and a few cuts and scratches later she had crossed it, making for the door of the shed. The door handle slipped in her hands as she attempted to open it. She tried it again, but it was locked.

She turned away from the thin dry strip along the edge of the building. After crossing the fence again, she continued along the road, the wind working against her. She held out her thumb, in the hope of a ride, trying to push out of her mind what had happened last time she had done this. Cars passed her, going in the opposite direction. Jess looked at the faces of the people inside. Some of them looked pityingly at her, but none of them stopped. By the time she reached the town again there wasn't a dry part on her body. Her hair clung to her face and sent cold drops down her neck. She found a retreat in the form of a tin shelter made for livestock in a double block between houses. She sat shivering uncontrollably, watching the rain outside. Her teeth chattered, and she gripped her knees tightly to her chest.

The rain continued into the evening and persisted all

night. Jess sat curled in a ball in the corner of the shelter. She couldn't sleep. She should have felt hungry too but all she could think about was her desperately cold body, trembling the night away.

The morning dawned still and clear. The wildness of the night had drifted away to rage in another place. Jess emerged stiff and run down. Her throat was sore. The world looked so different after a heavy rainstorm. The smell in the air was the familiar mixture of freshness and dust that rain always left behind. The legacy of the night before lay in numerous large puddles by the curb, made possible by the unevenness of the streets and lack of an efficient drainage system. Jess wandered down the road. The morning air was icy. It was little comfort knowing that a bit later in the day the sun would begin to take the chill off the air.

She passed by the back of a corner store. It was still early and some freshly delivered crates of milk stood by the door, not yet taken inside. They represented food — nourishment. She considered this for a moment. She was hungry, but more than that, she was desperately thirsty. Her tongue stuck to the insides of her mouth.

She looked around briefly to make sure there was no one around then swiftly grabbed a bottle and disappeared around the side of the building and into the overgrown garden of a neighbouring house. She uncapped the bottle and lifted it to her lips. The milk was icy cold, and felt good as it washed down her throat, making her body tingle. Discarding the bottle in the bushes she moved quickly on her way, in case anyone had seen her. It had all only taken about a minute.

Feeling vaguely better, Jess made her way into the centre of town. Her next priority was to get as far away as possible from this place. She would have to improve on her previous attempt. She continued to walk along the street.

As she passed the bus stop, a bus pulled in behind her. Impulsively, she turned towards it. The bus was run down and looked like it was in dire need of a service, but she couldn't afford to be fussy. It would take her where she wanted to go, which was anywhere but where she was. The driver glanced lifelessly at her and several other people who boarded before her. The bus pulled away from the curb. Jess went to the back and sat down on the back seat between an old woman and a dull, shabby looking man who was listening to music through headphones and staring straight ahead. His jaws moved up and down, chewing on a piece of gum. Jess felt uncomfortable. Her clothes were still damp. They stuck to her body. She had to hold onto the edges of the seat to stop herself sliding forward, lubricated by the dampness, every time the driver stepped on the brake.

Jess eyed the other people in the bus, which was about half full. Several sat contentedly reading a book or newspaper, oblivious to those around them. Most though, stared straight ahead or out of the window, expressionless, like zombies. From looking at them Jess could not tell if they were happy or sad. Like she, they were merely there in order to reach some destination, but hers was far less certain. She hadn't any idea where she was being taken.

Jess couldn't relax. Her muscles were tense. The dryness had returned to her throat. She swallowed painfully. She looked past the other people on the back seat and out the window. It soon became apparent that the bus was heading out of the town. *This is good*, she thought. The white posts with their red reflector strips flew past. When she was little and travelling in her parent's car, she would make a game out of those posts. She would see how many times she could tap her fingers or count to five before they reached the next white post. Now each one was simply a symbol of the growing distance between her and the Pullins.

But still she could not relax. She thought of them searching for her. She wondered what John had told Margi. Probably nothing. Would they be frantic? No, they were probably glad to be rid of her. They were probably laughing at her. She narrowed her eyes and tried to hold back the tears. She watched the mileage signs flash by at intervals along the road, telling her they were nearing another town. A man who had been chatting to the driver turned around and began to walk down the aisle. He wore a yellow reflector vest and carried a money box by a strap around his neck. A ticket inspector! He began at the front, checking other peoples' tickets. When he reached Jess, she shook her head.

'I don't have one.'

'Why not?'

'I forgot.'

'You can buy one now then.'

'Um, no.'

He looked down at her.

'I don't have any money.'

'Why are you riding on this bus then, eh?' He was firm but not harsh. He seemed to enjoy his authority. Jess didn't know what to say. She knew people were watching her.

'I'm sorry, you'll have to get off at the next stop.'

'How will I get home?'

'That's not my problem.' He shrugged.

It was not as far as she had hoped, but it didn't really matter, this place was as good as any other. The sign on the way into town read, WELCOME TO STANLEY CREEK, POPULATION 15,000. Jess knew of this place, she had been here once before. Her stomach began to growl. It had been empty for almost two days. The exposure had taken its toll and she felt sick and tired. It had been easy enough with the milk bottle that morning. Surely she could get something to eat the same way — or almost. It would require just a bit more skill. She knew plenty about picking window locks. She'd done it many times at home when her mother was away, and her father was too drunk to let her inside after school. All she would have to do was find one she knew how to open. She would only take some food, enough to get her by. It wasn't as if she was going to trash the place, or even take anything valuable. She tried to justify herself. She'd told herself that she'd only ever resort to this if she was desperate. She was. But break and enter? It sounded so criminal.

Wandering down a sleepy side street the proposition seemed less hopeful. All the houses were built close together and endorsed towering fences. There was only a small gate providing entrance to most, and some carried the warning: *BEWARE OF THE DOG.* Jess passed a gate with an outline drawing of a snarling bull terrier nailed firmly to it. *ENTER AT OWN RISK*, the words next to it read. Jess kicked a stone in annoyance and it went skidding along the cement. Immediately a chorus of barking came from behind the barriers.

The next street along looked a little more promising — more like the country town that it was. She only needed to slip down the side of a house where it looked like there was nobody home, and into the backyard. This normally would have been no problem at all, but Jess's eyes came to rest on a group of boys, spread out along the road, kicking a football. She watched them for a minute or two, deciding what to do. What if one of them saw her? What if the house she chose was one of theirs? It was too dangerous.

As she scouted street after street she became more apprehensive, and less and less sure that this was a good idea. Everywhere there was something wrong, something to deter her — a car in the drive, a neighbour's car, signs of a security system, or simply too conspicuous. Perhaps she was just stalling. Maybe she didn't have the courage to break into somebody's house. Even if she did, she knew she would only do it once. What then? She didn't want to think about the future.

Jess had reached the centre of town. Her boredom took her into the nearby shopping centre. She felt completely out of place amid the relative glitter and glamour of the small-town department store. She felt self-conscious and thought that politeness was all that prevented the shoppers from holding their noses as they passed her. She escaped back onto the street where she felt more at ease. Footpaths were strangely beginning to feel like home to her.

She passed a news stand and glanced at the news headlines and notices pinned to the billboard, where something caught her eye and she came to an abrupt stop. She had seen her name on one of those signs. Walking closer to the board, she scanned it until she came across a small notice in the far corner: *HAVE YOU SEEN JESS?* The bold black letters stared her in the face. Below them was a small reproduced black and white photograph of Jess's face, and the phone numbers of the Pullins, the department and the police. Jess hadn't the faintest idea where they'd found the photo of her. She had left all such identity with her parents and couldn't remember having her photo taken since.

'Oh my God,' she breathed. She stood and stared at it for a moment or two.

'Can I help you?'

Jess jumped in fright and spun around to face the friendly smile of the news stand attendant who stood close behind her.

'No thanks,' she said quickly. In a moment she had passed him and disappeared amongst the other people on the street, leaving him standing in front of the noticeboard.

Jess walked briskly along the pavement, and as she did so, reached up and pulled from her hair the band that held it in a pony tail, since that was how it had been worn in the photograph. She wasn't going to play into the hands of anyone who might recognise her.

Jess went to sleep that night in an un-locked garage, which seemed more inviting than a bus shelter. She had no difficulty in falling asleep this time, for her lack of nourishment made her feel lethargic and tired, and her heart as well as her stomach was empty.

Jess woke with a fever. Even before she sat up from the pile of hessian bags that she'd slept on, she could feel the throbbing pain of a headache. Her nose was blocked, forcing her to breathe through her mouth. When she did sit up, dizziness filled her head, her vision turned dark green and her stomach felt nauseated and hollow. Somehow, she managed to stagger outside, tripping over paint cans and other debris on the way. She steadied herself against the garage door before continuing down the driveway.

No one had seen her emerge, and it was probably just as well, because she wasn't capable of putting up much of a fight. She sat down at a picnic table on the lawns in front of a bowling club and put her head in her hands. She stayed there for most of the day, not having the strength or will to go anywhere. As the hours wore on, she felt worse and was beginning to contemplate doing something drastic.

Jess remembered that a girl from her school had once run away and lived on virtually nothing for several weeks. When she was found she was so badly run down and suffering so much from exposure that they couldn't save her in hospital. Jess didn't really want to die. She hadn't eaten a meal since lunch the day John had beaten her, and the prospect of another one wasn't looking good. She pictured herself starving in the middle of town, right outside dozens of shops full of food, amongst people who were too busy to care. A middle-aged woman walking a small white dog passed her at that moment.

'Excuse me,' Jess said. The woman turned to look at her. 'Can you spare a couple dollars? I need to catch the bus.' The woman's expression changed.

'Sorry,' she muttered softly, and tugged on the leash to extract the dog from something it had found to sniff on the ground. They hurried away. Another couple of people passed. Jess tried again but got a similar response.

She remained where she was, trying to tell herself she was better off than with the Pullins, but somehow couldn't believe it. Her head lay against the hard wood of the picnic table. Every throb of her head seemed to pound her whole body. Her breath came in short laboured gasps.

She was faced with a decision she didn't want to make. She wrestled with her thoughts. There was only one thing left to do. Carefully she stood up from the hard seat. She swayed and then established her balance before relinquishing her grip on the table. For several seconds she couldn't see the ground in front of her. Her vision cleared, revealing the littered grounds of the public park. Jess began to walk across the grass, compelled forward only by a desire to relieve her discomfort.

She didn't have to walk very far. The North Districts Hospital was a dark brick building, set back slightly from the street. She hesitated outside, struggling to come to grips with what she was about to do — to sacrifice her freedom, and to walk back onto the turnstile that was so hard to stop.

She went in the main entrance. The reception area was empty apart from a woman behind the desk. Jess stood just inside the door for a moment, letting her eyes grow accustomed to the relative gloom compared to the bright sunshine outside. Jess walked slowly up to the desk and collected herself to speak. The woman addressed her first.

'How can I help you?'

Jess couldn't answer. She had fainted.

CHAPTER 10

The smell of clean starched sheets and the high-pitched sound of hospital units were the first things that confronted Jess's senses as she awoke. Even before she opened her eyes she knew where she was. She felt the welcome warmth and softness of the bed surrounding her and relaxed her body.

When she opened her eyes, all she could see was the far wall and part of the ceiling which was painted a creamy grey. She lifted her head slightly off the pillow and suddenly the pain returned. Her head felt heavy. In fact, all her limbs felt stiff and heavy — as though they had occupied the same position for hours. Jess turned her head on the pillow, first to the left, to see the complicated-looking machine that was emitting the high regular tones that she could hear. She put her hands up to her face and discovered that there was a plastic tube running from her nose and a cannula in the back of her hand. She felt a pang of fear. *Why was all this stuff necessary? What was wrong?*

Turning her head in the other direction she saw another bed. It was empty, with the blanket folded neatly at the base, ready for some other victim of life.

Jess closed her eyes again. She couldn't remember anything of what happened after she'd walked into the hospital that day — or was it yesterday? The room didn't have a clock.

The silence was broken by the sound of brisk footsteps coming along the corridor outside the room. A moment later the door opened and a small thin nurse appeared. She had a round freckled face and blonde hair, piled high in a curly pony tail. The light blue uniform she wore looked tight and restricting.

The nurse walked up to Jess's bed.

'Oh good, you're awake,' she said. Jess could see the name tag on the nurse's breast — 'Valerie'. Valerie walked over to the window and flung open the curtains. Jess squinted in the light.

'How are you feeling?' she asked Jess.

'Okay, I guess.' Jess didn't really know how to answer because she wasn't sure how she felt. Valerie came over to the bedside and began adjusting the unit.

'What's that supposed to do?' Jess asked.

'It's an ECG, to monitor your heart while you were unconscious. That's your heart beat on the screen,' the nurse said, pointing to an oscillating disturbance on a small monitor. Watching her heart beat, Jess felt suddenly and strangely detached from her body, like an onlooker to her own life.

'Was I unconscious?'

'Yes, for about a day.'

'What about the tubes and stuff?' Jess fingered them.

'It's oxygen to help you breathe and a glucose and electrolyte solution,' the nurse said of each of the contraptions in turn.

'You mean I could have stopped breathing?' Jess asked in horror.

'Yes, you almost did.'

Then came the real question she wanted to ask. 'What's wrong with me?'

Valerie looked at her solemnly, then answered. 'Cuts and bruising, dehydration, mild concussion, and an acute case of viral pneumonia.' She rattled off Jess's afflictions one after another, counting them off on her fingers. Before Jess could respond, she asked curiously, 'What happened to you anyway?'

Jess didn't want to answer the question truthfully, so she didn't answer at all. She folded her arms and lay in silence.

'Well?' Valerie said expectantly.

'Does it matter?' Jess barked, her exterior suddenly growing defensive again.

'Mysterious, aren't you?' the nurse said. 'I'll just check your temp and BP then go and tell the doctor you've woken up.'

A while later, a large stocky man, who didn't look a bit like a doctor, came in.

'Hi, how are you feeling today?'

'Okay I guess,' Jess said, answering him in the same way she'd answered the nurse.

'Good to hear,' he said heartily. Jess felt like the last thing she needed was a cheerful doctor. He went to the foot of her bed, where he picked up her card. Jess noticed that there was already plenty of writing on it, but the top of the card was blank. There were no personal details on it.

After doing a brief examination the doctor pulled a chair up to the side of the bed. 'Do you feel up to having a little chat?'

Jess shrugged her shoulders.

'You didn't have any ID on you, but the hospital checked the missing person's list with the police — just as a matter of routine.'

Jess sat silently. She knew what was coming.

'Are you Jessica Dimitri?'

She gave a brief reluctant nod. She knew it was useless now.

'Since we've sorted that out, I'm sure you wouldn't mind telling me about these bruises.' He pointed to the ugly blue and red patches on Jess's face.

'I don't feel well. I don't want to talk,' Jess said, excusing herself from the question.

'Maybe I'll come back later then, when you're feeling a bit better,' he said cooperatively. 'You get some rest.' Jess thought she detected a tone of mockery in his voice, as though he knew she was only avoiding his interrogation.

'Do you want the curtains shut?' the doctor asked.

'Yeah, whatever.'

Jess closed her eyes, but she didn't rest. She began debating with herself how much she should tell of what John had done to her. After a while she decided she might as well tell them everything. She had nothing more to lose. She wasn't like Olivia, for whom she knew there would be ramifications. They couldn't make her go back to live with them after this. Maybe John would go to jail.

The next morning, after an unappetising breakfast of

something Jess couldn't identify, the doctor came to examine her. She was propped up by numerous pillows. The drip line and tubes had been removed and she was breathing on her own, but still with difficulty. The day was Saturday, two days after she had turned herself in. Already she felt as though she'd been in hospital for a lifetime. She had not left her bed except for several staggered trips down the hall to the bathroom.

'Bed pans are not exactly my style,' she had firmly informed the nurse. The hospital staff had come to realise her stubbornness and disregard for doctor's orders.

Jess had never been in hospital before, and she felt out of place in the sterile atmosphere. The hospital gown she wore was several sizes too big and seemed more suited to the maternity ward. Jess found herself constantly pulling it down as it rode up her legs as she lay in bed, by virtue of its open-backed style.

The doctor told her that her condition was improving rapidly, considering her body's low immunity.

'What you have is a pneumonia caused by a virus which you've probably had for several days. It is an infection of the lung tissue. The resulting inflammation causes blocking of the alveoli; the lung tissue becomes consolidated, and oxygen cannot pass through to the blood in that region. Antibiotics are usually of no value with virus infected tissue. Recovery should be spontaneous. However, a lung infected by a virus may be more easily infected by bacteria, which is sometimes a complication. My prognosis at this stage is that with continued rest and surveillance you will be back to good Health in a short time. I'd say you'll be out of here within a week.' The doctor ended his exposition. Jess hadn't really been listening to his technical description of her illness until he came to the last sentence.

'A *week*!' she cried. A further protest would have followed but a bout of wheezed coughing prevented her from speaking. She sank down onto her pillows, her chest heaving to force the air through her lungs.

'Well, where else have you got to go?' He eyed her sharply as if to remind her of their talk the previous day.

Just then, a voice sounded over the intercom in the corridor, calling the doctor to casualty. He left with his statement fresh in Jess's mind. She frowned. But it was nothing she didn't already know.

In the middle of the week, the nurse told Jess that a representative from the department was coming to see her. She didn't like this prospect. She envisaged that all they would do was pretend to want to help her, ask hundreds of questions, then send her back to Wellingwood. Jess wasn't looking forward to it, but she knew there was no way out. Another escape plan flickered briefly through her mind, but she gave it up immediately as futile.

A man arrived the following morning. It was Friday. He wore a black shirt and pants. Jess thought he looked like he was dressed for a funeral, which she thought was rather appropriate.

'Hello,' he greeted her as he sat down. His neatly parted hair shone in the sun that streamed through the window. 'I'm Thomas, from the Department of Family and Community Services. I'm here to discuss the recent events with your foster family and to talk about where to go from here.'

'Hello,' Jess said without interest.

'Feeling better?'

'Yes, physically,' she said, not really knowing why.

'Oh, and what about emotionally?' the man asked, beginning a flow of careful and obviously prepared questions. Jess shrugged her shoulders.

'I've spoken to your foster mother. She says her husband hit you while she was out. I need your side of the story.'

'There's nothing much to tell. He beat me up. He's a mongrel.' Jess spoke with enmity as she remembered the encounter.

'So, you ran away?'

'Wouldn't *you*?'

'I would have told somebody, and tried to work it out, but that doesn't matter now,' he reasoned. Jess marvelled. He had no idea of what it was like.

'I can tell you right now that I am *not* going back there,' she said with determination.

'That would be wise.'

'What?' Jess said, wondering if she'd heard correctly.

'Jess, my job is to make sure you have a sound home to live in. It's obvious that the Pullins can't provide you with that at the moment. Other arrangements will have to be made.'

At that moment, Jess felt an enormous weight lifted from her. She couldn't believe what she was hearing. Never again would she have to face John, and never again look at Olivia's scornful face.

'Thank you,' she breathed, not knowing what else to say.

'It's my pleasure. I'll arrange to have your things picked up.'

'But what then?' Jess was still confused. The man scratched his chin.

'Another home will have to be found for you — another family.'

Jess's heart sank slightly, but she knew she didn't have much choice. Still, it was better than going back to Wellingwood — marginally. Her thoughts turned to Margi. How did she find out? What was she going to do now that she knew about John?

'Why hasn't Margi been to see me?' she asked.

'I advised her not to, until I'd spoken to you. Why, do you want her to?'

'Not particularly.'

When he had gone, Jess felt a surge of relief. The meeting had gone much better than she'd anticipated, but now she had to go through everything again with another family. She braced herself for the experience.

About mid-morning the following day Jess's door opened, and the now-familiar nurse Valerie walked in. Jess had been curiously watching the patient in the bed next to her. The middle-aged woman was engrossed in unwrapping the gifts she'd received. Jess didn't know why this woman was in hospital, but suspected it was one of those things that tended to happen as a person gets older. She had been inundated with flowers and gifts, and her bedside table was already covered in *Get Well* cards. It contrasted violently to Jess's table, which was bare apart from her glass of water, and gathered only dust.

'You have a visitor,' Jess heard the nurse say.

Another one! How many relatives did this woman have?

'Jess, there's someone here to see you.'

Jess looked up.

'Me?' she said, the surprise showing in her voice. Why couldn't people from the department leave her alone?

'Shall I send her in?'

'Sure, go ahead. What else have I got to lose?' Jess mumbled the last sentence. The nurse disappeared and a minute later her visitor stood inside the door.

'Jess.'

Jess looked up and her stomach suddenly flipped.

'Margi,' she said.

'Hello — you look a mess,' Margi said anxiously.

'Still.'

'I'm so sorry. I'm just so sorry,' she cried, releasing her tension and rushing over to Jess's bed, but she didn't dare hug her, for she must have known the reaction that would bring.

'I know John can be a bit temperamental, especially when he's — well you know — but I wouldn't have thought—oh,

Jess, I'm so glad you're all right.' Jess sat looking down at her hands. She felt uncomfortable.

Margi continued. 'Olivia is worried about you.'

'Yeah, *sure* she is.'

'She was outraged at John when she heard what had happened. I've never seen her so angry. She let out many things that I just had no idea about.'

Jess was surprised at this but was sure Olivia had only been angry because Margi knew about him now. She didn't have to hide it anymore.

'But how did you find out? John didn't tell you.' She was still confused.

'He said he'd taught you a lesson. Olivia knew what that meant. Besides, he was still drunk, and we all know what *that* means.' Margi was finding it difficult to speak. There were tears in her eyes. 'It hurts me that my own daughter couldn't tell me what had been happening all that time. I didn't suspect anything. I should have, he's been giving me hell for years, but— oh, Jess, if only I'd known ...' Margi paused to look sadly at her. Jess became aware of the patient next to her, who was watching them curiously. She had stopped examining her gifts.

'Olivia said she knew if he ever hit you there would be trouble,' Margi said. A thought struck Jess. Maybe Olivia was hoping he would turn on her, so it would all be out in the open. She had known Jess wouldn't keep quiet about it.

'John is going to live with his mother for the time being, so you can come back. It will all be different now. Please come back,' Margi pleaded. Jess shook her head.

'You know I can't,' she said, not wanting to look at Margi's face.

'I don't blame you for being upset, but I don't want to lose you because of this,' Margi sobbed. Jess couldn't believe it. She was talking as if what had happened was just a temporary falling out.

'I'm not coming back to live with you,' she said. 'And I don't think they'll let me anyway,' she added, seeing the distraught expression on Margi's face. 'I'm sorry …' she said softly.

Jess felt suddenly sorry for her. It was perhaps the first time in her life that she'd pitied someone else. Prior to this, it had always been anger, hatred or fear. It was strange. She didn't like this new feeling. It was almost like guilt, but she had nothing to feel guilty about. Neither had Margi though. What was going to happen to her now?

Margi clasped her hands tensely in her lap.

'Please, Jess, *please*,' she said. The hope was still in her voice. Jess shook her head.

'You're like a child to me — I — I love you.' Jess sat still, with an unmoved expression on her face. She didn't lift her eyes from the blankets in front of her.

'Please …' Margi's voice squeaked. Jess did not respond. A few silent minutes passed, then Jess heard Margi get up. Her footsteps retreated slowly towards the door.

'Goodbye then, Jess.' Margi turned and disappeared out into the long hospital corridor. It was a goodbye that would perhaps be forever.

Jess wiped away a tear that had lodged itself in her nose groove. She looked over at the woman beside her. She was pretending to look at a pack of fancy soaps, but the look on her face was a mixture of horror and pity. Jess turned away to face the other wall.

Two days later, the man from the department returned with the news that a new foster home had been found.

'Robert and Erica Bowman. They are very keen to take you in,' he told her.

'You must not have told them much about me,' Jess said dryly.

'You're not that bad. Besides, these people will be able to handle you. They're very experienced in the field of parenting — very nice people.'

'That's what they said last time.'

'I think this time you'll find it to be true. They already have a foster daughter as well as four other children, so I think they've proved themselves. It's important for this to get off to a good start. You have to put in some effort, Jess.'

Jess didn't feel like making much of an effort to do anything. Everything seemed so pointless. Sometimes she wondered whether it was worth fighting them all. She knew, though, that she was also fighting herself. No new person or place was going to make any difference.

CHAPTER 11

The Bowman's house was situated in a quiet part of Stonewell, a town not far from where the Pullins lived. It was built on a spacious block of land, with wide green lawns both front and back. The house was modern and had large front windows with the blinds partly drawn. The garden was immaculate. There was a small fish pond in the corner of the front yard, shimmering in the sunlight of the unseasonably warm afternoon. It all looked very stylish to Jess, compared to the plain exterior of the Pullin's home. Jess, accompanied by the usual social worker, walked up the wide cement driveway. The front door was a dark expensive looking wood, with narrow frosted glass panels. A wind chime sang sleepily above their heads. A knock on the door was answered almost immediately by a woman. She looked energetic and seemed happy to see them.

'Hello, I'm Erica. It's lovely to meet you Jess.'

Once inside, she turned her back on them and called out. 'Jess is here everybody.'

Suddenly, from every direction, people emerged from the other rooms of the house. They stood together in a bunch in the entrance hall. Jess counted them, there were six — seven including the woman. Their faces looked inquisitive but friendly. One by one, Jess's new foster mother introduced the family.

'This is my husband Robert, our children — Ben, Lisah, Serena, Ginger and Kate.' She looked proud of her family.

The first person Jess looked at was Robert. He was wearing a dark tailored suit. He must have an important job, she thought. An office job probably. He most likely had taken time off work to be home when Jess arrived. He was lean and well groomed, with dark hair. He bore no physical resemblance to John. Jess was secretly relieved.

Ben was a plump red-headed boy. Jess was later to find out that he was sixteen, and a year ahead of her at school. Both Lisah and Serena looked a little younger than herself. They stood next to each other. Their looks were very different. Lisah had short light brown hair and Serena, longer, darker hair. Lisah had freckles on her face and arms, like her brother. Serena was perhaps the prettier of the two. Jess decided that she must be the foster daughter as she didn't look like anyone else in the family.

The twins, Ginger and Kate, were about eight years old and looked so alike that Jess wondered how she was going to be able to tell them apart. They had straight ash coloured hair, pulled back in the same fashion. Their faces were small and sweet. Jess wondered what it was going to be like living with such a multitude.

Jess sat near one end of the long dining table, which was needed to accommodate the large family. Kate sat next to Jess but had her back to her, engaged in a conversation with Ginger. The pair had little to say to the rest of the family for the entire meal. They were obviously great friends and caught up in their own world.

Jess ate quietly, not speaking unless she was spoken to, which meant she didn't say much at all. The family seemed to be treating her as one of them already, giving her no more attention than the others seated around the table. Jess had been prepared to be bombarded with family news and customs and expected a lot of questions about herself and her previous family. In a way she was relieved that the attention was not on her, but at the same time felt strange — as though she was only partly there. The Bowmans might have thought of Jess as part of the family, but she couldn't feel a part of it. As the meal wore on she began to lose her appetite and toyed with the food on her plate, pushing it back and forth with her fork. Several times she noticed Erica snatch a glance across the table at her and her unfinished meal. Jess could feel the beginnings of a headache creeping through her brain.

'May I be excused?' she said, and added, 'I don't feel well, I must still have pneumonia or something.'

'Yes, sure.'

Jess left the table and retreated to her new bedroom. She closed the door and sat down on the bed. It was quite firm and covered with a plain brown quilt. She gave a little bounce to see if it squeaked the way her bed at the Pullins had. It didn't. Looking around the room, she noticed how bare the walls were. The walls at the Pullin's house had been covered with homely things. Even in her parents' house there were cheap paintings on every wall. Perhaps she was supposed to decorate the room herself.

Earlier that day Lisah had shown her to the room. She told her that if it smelled strange it was because they'd had it sprayed for cockroaches before Jess arrived. Jess didn't know whether to believe her or not. Lisah was pleasant and talkative, and seemed to want to help Jess arrange the room. Jess didn't show any willingness to accept the offer so Lisah had left her alone in the room, which was where she stayed almost until dinnertime.

Jess stood up and walked over to the window and looked out at the large backyard. There was a trampoline and a swing set on the lawn. In the corner of the yard an old car tyre hung from a large willow tree. There was no back fence. She watched a black and white cat walk gracefully along the ridge poll of the neighbour's roof. Jess stood by the window for some time. She was thinking — about the kindness already shown to her by the Bowmans, and the way they seemed to understand how she felt by allowing her to leave the table. Her thoughts began to drift back to the Pullins.

Throughout the day, she'd found herself comparing every aspect of this new family and home to them. The comparison was sometimes favourable and sometimes not. She didn't think she liked the idea of having so many brothers and sisters, although maybe it would mean less individual attention, which appealed to her. She couldn't understand why anyone would want so many children. The thought crossed her mind that perhaps they were only having her so that they could collect the allowance from the government at the end of the week. This thought began to sprout other doubts in her mind. What if they made her do all the housework and baby-sit the twins? Robert didn't seem like the kind of man who would beat his children. Jess couldn't trust him all the same. The worst types were often well disguised.

'I can't trust any of them,' she whispered. Jess was brought back to the present by a knock on the door. It was Ben who stood outside it.

'We're going down to the youth club, do you want to join us?' he asked.

'Who's we?'

'Lisah, Serena and me.'

Jess paused before answering. 'No — thanks.'

'Are you sure? You could meet some of the kids from school.'

'I just want to stay here and get organised tonight.'

'Well if you're sure.'

'You go, it's okay.'

'All right. We'll see you tomorrow then I guess.'

'Yeah.'

Ben left, closing the door behind him. Jess stood where she was, pondering the smile he had given her. It was an understanding smile. She walked back over to her bed and lay down on top of the quilt, with her hands folded across her chest. She felt worse than ever now.

That night Jess dreamed she was inside the Pullin's house,

like a soul floating through the rooms. She could hear Olivia screaming, and could see John at the top of the stairs. He was drunk. Margi was crouched behind a chair. She was speaking in a frantic voice, but Jess couldn't make out the words. No matter how hard she tried, she could not make out the words.

'Mum have you seen my purple top?' Lisah's voice floated through the house.

'Can I have some money for a Geography excursion?'

'Are you watching the eggs, Kate? They're going to burn.' Early morning chaos reigned in the Bowman household. From her room Jess could hear every word spoken, or rather shouted, in the mad dash to be on time for school and work.

Jess emerged just as quick goodbyes were being said before everyone disappeared out the door. The chatter died away and the house was quiet again. Jess looked over at Erica, who was tidying up the breakfast dishes. She wore no makeup at all. Her chestnut coloured hair was short and simply styled.

Is it always this noisy in the mornings?' Jess asked.

'Yes. You'll get used to it. I guess you're accustomed to nice quiet mornings, the way nature intended it to be I suppose.'

Jess shrugged her shoulders. She didn't know if she wanted to get used to it. She didn't know if this was going to work out.

Jess spent the day in town with Erica, shopping for clothes and other necessities. Despite herself, she enjoyed getting new things. She hadn't been shopping for a long time, so the experience was a novelty. She'd been used to not having many possessions ever since she'd stopped living with her parents. At first, she had missed some of her favourite things and often wondered what had happened to them. Now though, she barely owned anything, and certainly nothing of any value. Clothes weren't important to her. She didn't care what she wore. While most teenagers saw clothes as a statement of who they were — or at least who they wanted to be — that was not Jess. Her mild fashion sense had given way to practicality long ago.

Later that afternoon Jess discovered that she was expected to go to school the next day. Robert and Erica saw no reason for her to stay at home any longer than she needed to settle in, which they considered she'd already had.

Wearing her new uniform and carrying her bag over her shoulder, Jess followed the Deputy Headmaster of Stonewell State High School down the corridor of the Year Ten block. He stopped outside a door with the number **10 A1** painted on it in small black print and after giving a firm brisk knock, he entered with an authority that only someone of such status would dare. He gestured for Jess to follow. She did, being unable to control the butterflies that were leaping around inside of her.

The classroom was small and crammed with desks, behind which sat students, laughing and talking noisily amongst themselves. None of them seemed to notice Jess at first, but when they saw the Deputy Headmaster, some of them turned curiously to face the front. A male teacher sat behind the desk at the side of the room, talking to the Deputy.

Jess didn't think he looked like the kind of man who'd be able to relate to teenagers. As she was being introduced to the class, Jess looked at each face in turn. Many of their jaws were going up and down, chewing gum. They were all watching her inquisitively. Jess was directed to an empty seat near the front. The eyes were all still on her. She moved the chair back just enough to fit between it and the desk. Just as she started to sit down she noticed one of the straps from her bag caught around the leg of the chair. She lifted her weight and yanked at it, but as she did so the tilted chair slid on the waxed wooden floor and out from under her. She crashed to the floor in an ungraceful heap. The room was filled with shrieks of hysterical laughter. Hurriedly, she picked herself up. She could feel her face burning red.

Jess repositioned the chair and sat down carefully, dropping her bag on the floor beside her. She threw a brief look back at the other students who weren't making any effort to hide their amusement. The giggles and snickers died away as the teacher called the class to order. Jess sat hunched in her seat. She wished she was somewhere else and fixed her eyes firmly on the desk.

Jess spent most of the morning in the office, waiting for her timetable to be processed. Jess thought time had passed slowly while she was in hospital, but it was nothing compared to sitting alone in that tiny stuffy office. What annoyed her most was the office staff, who from time to time came in with the encouraging news, 'Shouldn't be long now,' then left her waiting for another half hour until someone else came to repeat the message. She could faintly hear the bell that signalled the end of lessons for the other students. She thought she counted four or five of them.

Jess ate her lunch alone on a seat outside the library. She watched the small groups of girls sitting in gossiping circles on the lawn. When the bell rang she pulled out the crumpled piece of paper that told her which lesson she was supposed to attend. After several minutes of trying to sort out the codes and numbers on the timetable, Jess went to look for Room fifteen, which, as far as she could work out, was where she had Geography with Mr Zelic in that period. She found Room nine and followed the row of buildings. When the buildings ended at the sports field, Jess stopped. She was up to Room thirteen. She stood for a moment and looked around. The yard was becoming deserted as people disappeared into classrooms.

Beginning to panic, she turned around and walked back the way she had come. As she rounded the corner of the next block a figure flew towards her, colliding with her roughly. When both had recovered, the tall, dark-haired boy bent down to pick up Jess's bag.

'Sorry, I'm late for class, I wasn't watching where I was going,' he said bashfully. 'Hey, you were in my home class this morning, weren't you? You're new.'

'Yeah, unfortunately — being new that is.' Jess couldn't remember his face. It was slender and quite good looking.

'Um, can you tell me where Room fifteen is?' she asked, seizing the opportunity.

'Yeah, I'm going down that way, I'll take you there.'

He led her across the courtyard to an orange door.

'See ya later,' the boy said, and vanished around the corner. Jess went in. The rest of the class was already seated. She was accosted by a partly balding teacher wearing bifocals.

'Yes?' he said impatiently. Jess was taken aback.

'I think I'm supposed to be in this class. I just got here today,' she said, matching his tone.

'Aren't you a bit late?' he snapped.

'I couldn't find the room,' Jess said unapologetically.

'Is that my problem?'

'No, but I—'

He cut her off, 'Just go and sit down, I've had just about enough from you kids for one day.'

Jess marched over to the nearest empty desk, kicking a bag out of her way. She dumped her own on the floor and sat down noisily.

'I am not in a good mood, so don't make me angry,' Mr Zelic said sternly. 'And if you're going to be part of my class you will be on time, is that clear?'

Jess didn't answer.

'Is that *clear*?' he bellowed.

'*Yes!*' she half shouted back at him. He looked at her disapprovingly. When he walked back over to his desk, Jess dropped her head onto her own desk with a loud thud, not caring whether she was being looked at.

Mr Zelic stood at the front of the room for most of the lesson, talking about the South American rain forests. He pointed to maps on the wall and waved his hands animatedly about. Jess sat thinking of animals in the zoo that he resembled and how much she hated his green spotted tie. About midway through the lesson, Jess looked up unexpectedly when he asked her a question.

'I don't know,' she said.

'Have you been listening?' the teacher demanded. She hadn't.

'Yes,' she replied.

'Then will you kindly answer the question please.' He spoke to her slowly, as though she was a small child being urged to obey.

'I told you I don't know.'

'Why do I bother? Sometimes I really don't know why I bother.' He threw his hands in the air.

'It's not my fault you can't teach,' Jess ventured softly. Mr Zelic had heard her though.

'How did you make it to high school, young lady? Perhaps we should send you over to the kindergarten across the road.'

The class snickered. For the second time already that day Jess was the subject of the class entertainment. Her anger was building up. She couldn't take it any longer. She rose to her feet.

'You can stuff your stupid rain forests and you can stuff your stupid class!' she yelled. She stormed over to the door, turned the handle several times before it opened, then ran outside and away from them all.

She headed for the girls' toilet block. It was locked, with a sign on the door that said CLOSED FOR REPAIRS. This meant she had to make the trek across the other side of the school to the Physical Education toilet block, that she remembered from a brief tour that morning. She went into a cubicle and sat down on the closed seat. She had always hated teachers. In her mind they came into the same category as the Wellingwood people and the police.

Suddenly she realised she'd left her bag in the classroom. She'd have to go back later and get it. Jess couldn't wait for the day to come to an end.

CHAPTER 12

When Jess arrived home that afternoon, there was a sealed cardboard box on the kitchen table.

'Someone from the department dropped it off,' Erica told her. 'It's your things from your other foster home. I asked where the rest was, but she said that was all she was given.'

'That probably is the rest,' Jess said, walking over to the box and tearing off the tape. She lifted the flaps and peered inside. It contained her hessian backpack, some items of clothing and a few odds and ends. She realised she owned even less than she had thought. She picked up the box and carried it to her room. As she sifted through the contents she came across a small white piece of paper lying in the bottom of the box. She picked it up. It was a note, scribbled in black ink:

Dear Jess,
I'm sorry it had to end this way. It was never meant to be like this. One day when you think you're ready I hope you can come back to us and we can all start over again. Please keep in touch.
Love, Margi

As soon as she'd read it, Jess tore it up viciously and threw the pieces of paper across the room. They fluttered to the floor like snowflakes.

'Why can't they just leave me alone?' she cried. She so desperately wanted to escape the memories of the last few weeks. She looked down at a small china puppy that lay on the bed. Margi had given it to her when she'd arrived. She picked it up and cupped it in her hand, surveying it. After several moments she went over and put it in the bottom of the wardrobe, then did the same with the other things that were in the box. She folded the clothes and put them away in a drawer.

Jess ran her fingers down the column of her timetable, studying it carefully. She didn't have Geography until second to last period that day, which was straight after lunch. She was glad, and hoped Mr Zelic wasn't at school that day.

Jess was sitting alone in a row of three desks in her home room that morning. The boy she'd bumped into the day before sat across the aisle from her. His name was Mark Traicos. She knew that because it was written on the cover of one of his books, which lay on the corner of his desk. He seemed like a friendly enough person, and very popular as well.

After the bulletin notices had been read out, everybody crowded out the door and wandered off to their classes. Jess's first lesson that day was Health. She remembered the teacher setting some homework questions which she'd not attempted. As she approached the classroom her mind was active, conjuring up an excuse. She was relieved that she had a female teacher for Health. Perhaps she would be more lenient than one of her male colleagues had been the day before. She hoped to find her in a good mood.

Later, in the Phys. Ed change rooms, Jess pushed her way through the crowd of girls to a clear space on the bench at the far end. She hadn't played any sport for a long time. When she was younger she had been a good tennis player, and as children, she and her brother would often play cricket in the backyard with homemade bats. Any sporting prowess she possessed had since evaporated and given way to more necessary activities.

The class was nearing the end of a unit of hockey, a sport Jess had never liked much. When it came time for picking teams, Jess stood miserably clutching her stick, dreading being left to last. She wasn't last though. As one of the captains called her to his team, a girl who stood next to her gave her a nasty look and began whispering something to one of her friends, producing a rude giggle from the other girl. Jess didn't like these girls. They were snobbish and seemed to be looking down their noses at her. Jess had already developed the opinion that the entire female contingent of Stonewell High considered themselves the most stunning and irresistible specimens alive on the earth. She didn't need them as her friends.

As she went over to where the rest of the team stood, leaving the girls standing with the other unchosen players, she felt slightly uplifted. She suddenly felt compelled to make the most of the opportunity, and not give them any more chance to laugh at her.

Although Jess had never liked playing team sports much,

the lesson went satisfactorily. She even managed to score a goal, to the delight of her team mates. Walking back to the change rooms, she flicked her sweaty hair out of her face. Her legs were sore from the vigorous workout. Just then, a hockey stick shot out in front of her feet. She managed to dodge it. The owner of the stick appeared from behind her and stood in Jess's way, forcing her to stop dead. It was the same girl who had been whispering at the start of the lesson. Maybe Jess had imagined it, but when she had possession of the ball, the girl's tackles had been more aggressive and purposeful. She'd dismissed this extra competitiveness, using it to fuel her own motivation.

'Excuse me,' Jess said calmly.

'What the hell do you think you were doing out there?' the girl demanded.

'Playing hockey,' Jess replied flatly.

'Don't be smart. You were trying to hit on James, weren't you? I saw you. Just stay away from him, all right.' She pointed a finger fiercely in Jess's face.

'I wasn't trying to *hit* on anyone. Get out of my way!' Jess spat back.

'No way! You were trying to steal my—' her sentence was cut short as the curved end of Jess's hockey stick connected sharply with the girl's shin bone. Jess pushed past her and disappeared into the equipment shed.

At lunch time, Jess was confined to the classroom, doing her Health homework from the night before. The teacher had reprimanded her, saying that she was not getting off to a good start and that the work would have to be caught up during break time. She told Jess that she was at a disadvantage already, being a new student in the middle of the year, and she would have to work hard to catch up.

She sat at the desk in the empty classroom, staring at the pages of her text book. She had begun by reading through the questions and thought them totally irrelevant to anyone's life — especially hers. She sighed loudly and tipped back on the hind legs of her chair, chewing on her pen. She could hear people outside the room, but the high windows prevented her from seeing them. Jess gazed out the window, up at the trees and the sky, where fluffy white clouds merged and mingled with each other. Her mind was far away.

After several minutes, she brought it back and resigned herself to her work. The time ticked away slowly. Jess dropped her pen on the page and stretched her arms above her head. She looked up at the clock and suddenly realised she'd have to go to her Geography lesson with Mr Zelic in ten minutes. She found herself dreading walking into that classroom full of students who had laughed at her, and Mr Zelic's overbearing figure standing at the front with his hands on his hips. She tried to imagine what sarcastic comments he was going to use to make fun of her that day. She didn't want to face him again just yet. Suddenly a thought struck her — she didn't have to face him. She didn't have to do anything.

Quickly, she threw her books into her bag and got up from the desk. In a moment she was standing out in the school yard. She began to walk towards the eastern sports field, which marked the boundary of the school. A caravan park was on the other side of it. Jess looked around to make sure no one was watching, then crossed the field into the obscurity of the park.

She felt increasingly more at ease as she wandered through the rows of caravans and cabins. She came out onto the bank of a man-made lake where ducks floated peacefully on the water. Jess felt the way she had after escaping from Wellingwood. It was a relieved but excited feeling.

She looked at her watch. The afternoon lessons had just begun. She could imagine Mr Zelic asking the class where she was and being met with a blank response. She smiled to herself. *What a sucker*, she thought. Feeling freer than she had for quite a while, her exploring impulses took over, and in a very short time she'd forgotten all about school and Mr Zelic and the rest of her classes for that day.

The next morning, Jess was called to the Deputy's office. She knocked on the door and stood back, feeling confident and one step ahead of the school hierarchy. The previous night while lying in bed, she'd devised a story to explain her absence. She thought it was so convincing that even Miss Brooke at Wellingwood would have believed it. She didn't get a chance to use it though and emerged from the office several minutes later in a state of mild shock. She couldn't believe what she'd just heard. A student had reported her to the principal for assault with a hockey stick. Brianna McQuillan was the alleged victim of Jess's brutality. Jess's first reaction was to laugh, but the humour had quickly died away as she realised he was quite serious. She was given a chance to defend herself but wasn't certain she'd convinced him. A letter would be sent home to her foster parents.

'It was only a little tap,' Jess had protested to the Deputy who had answered:

'Violence in any form is not condoned at this school. It is unacceptable behaviour. I don't know what the rules were like where you came from, but I'm telling you what they are here.'

Jess had felt the overwhelming urge to punch him between his imposing little eyes but knew that it would not help her case at all.

At recess time, Jess tracked down the person responsible for the situation she was now in. She found Brianna sitting with some friends on the grass near the Home Economics centre in one of those small circles Jess detested. She strode up to the group and focused on her enemy. With her hands on her hips, she said, 'I'd like a word with you.'

The faces all turned toward the figure who stood over them.

'Well well well, look who it is, the hockey queen herself.'

Laughter followed, but not from Jess, who stood her ground.

'I guess you think you're pretty damn good, reporting me like that. You've got a real nerve,' she said. More laughter followed this remark.

'You deserved it. You can't just go around whacking people with hockey sticks.'

'If that hurt you then you're even more pathetic than I thought,' Jess retorted.

One of Brianna's friends joined in. 'You're a psycho. People like you should be locked up.' The words came from a small, meek looking girl. Jess turned to her.

'And who asked for your opinion?' she said quickly, the volume of her voice beginning to rise considerably. She gave the unsuspecting girl a hard shove with her knee.

'Leave her alone!' Brianna shouted.

'Make me!' Jess challenged.

Brianna, taking up the invitation, rose quickly to her feet. She was several centimetres taller than Jess.

'I'll make you all right.' She advanced on Jess, who stood where she was, waiting to see what Brianna would do. For several seconds both were like statues. The girls who still sat on the ground were watching, intrigued.

Brianna marched up to Jess and gave her a push, sending her backwards and off balance.

'You're going to have to do better than that,' Jess said. She saw she'd brought the anger to the surface and waited for it to overflow. It did — with a flying hand aimed at Jess's throat. Jess clenched her fists and struck back. Brianna's sharp finger nails dragged painfully across her skin. Jess groped for a limb to twist or break. The other girl savagely kicked and punched and bit. In a few seconds they were both on the ground.

A small crowd of interested spectators had begun to gather. Anything that brought some excitement was clearly welcome. As the contest intensified, the other students began cheering them on. By now neither girl was a pretty sight.

Just as Jess was starting to feel as though she was gaining

the upper hand, she felt herself being torn away by a pair of strong hands. A moment later she found herself eye to eye with her Maths teacher. The crowd fell silent and began to disperse. Jess glanced around her, unaware until just then of the attention they'd been drawing. She looked at Brianna. Her brown hair was ruffled, and her face was flushed. Her eyes were wild. Jess's own adrenaline was flowing. She couldn't stand still, but she couldn't move either because the hand held her tightly. The teacher didn't bother to say anything, but instead began leading them both towards the office building. Jess returned the stares she received as they passed the junior school block. She walked slowly, resisting the pressure. Brianna had given up, allowing herself to be led along limply.

They were deposited in the same office where Jess had been that morning. As soon as the two were alone, Brianna spoke. 'This is all your fault. I've never been in serious trouble in my life. My parents are going to kill me.'

'Well maybe now we're even,' said Jess.

The door opened and a figure familiar to Jess walked in. He looked first at her.

'You're becoming a rather frequent visitor to these parts,' he said.

'It's not my fault I'm cursed,' she answered back. He ignored this.

'Now that you're both here, maybe we can sort this whole thing out once and for all.'

At the end of the day Jess lingered at school for a while. She didn't want to have to walk home with Ben, Lisah or Serena. She walked slowly along the footpath. In her hand she held a letter from the principal. It not only contained news of the hockey stick incident, but a notice of suspension as well. Jess had received the same lecture several times now — how she 'wasn't getting off to a good start' and was 'branding herself as a trouble-maker'. She wasn't looking forward to going home that day. She had thought of destroying the letter, but she knew it was only a formality anyway. Whatever was going to happen would still happen, with or without the piece of paper.

CHAPTER 13

Jess was suspended for three days. She was relieved that she didn't have to go to school for a while, but it meant spending more time at home during the day with Erica, who didn't seem to have any kind of a job outside the home. She felt as though she was being monitored, even when Erica was in another part of the house, which she usually was since Jess spent most of the time in her room. Her apathy and inactivity while Erica went about her work, almost as if she wasn't there, made her feel slightly guilty. Everyone else in the family seemed so perfect, never putting a foot wrong.

Perhaps it was Jess's imagination, but they seemed to have changed towards her. Nobody talked very much about her enforced absence from school. Maybe they thought she wasn't worth their attention. From time to time Robert dropped a remark about what was expected of her. He put a positive spin on the situation by commenting on how much more time Jess would have to help around the house over the next few days. Jess marvelled over how Robert always seemed so relaxed and impassive, while still maintaining a suitable level of involvement in all his family's affairs.

The twins wanted to know every detail of what had happened and seemed to look upon Jess with a certain awe. Their behaviour caused her to shrink away from all of them, and increase her distance from the rest of the family. She spent more and more time in her room; it had become a sanctuary.

Early one evening she was sitting sideways in an arm chair in the living room with her feet resting up against the wall, paging through a television magazine. Ben came in and saw her there.

'That's last week's issue,' he said.

'It'd be all the same to me if it was last year's issue,' Jess replied lifelessly. He read into her tone.

'You're really hung up about this suspension thing, aren't you?'

'No. The less I see of old baboon-face the better,' she said.

Ben stifled a laugh. 'You mean Mr Zelic?'

'Mmm.'

There was a moment's silence.

'Who started the fight?' was Ben's next question, unable to hold back his curiosity.

'I don't know. It just sort of happened,' Jess said.

'You don't reveal much, do you?' Ben said, in an intimate but brotherly way. He sat down in the chair next to her.

'Where is everybody?' Jess asked, beginning to wish she didn't have to be alone with him.

'I don't know. Outside I guess.' He shrugged.

Jess began looking through the magazine again, but not taking much notice of what the pages contained. Ben stayed where he was.

'You know, I like you, Jess.'

Jess pretended she didn't hear him.

He continued. 'Serena says you're stuck up, but what would she know, right?'

Jess couldn't pretend she didn't hear *this*. 'What gives her the right to go talking about me behind my back?' she said in a sudden rising tone.

Ben smiled, raising his palms in front of him in a peace gesture. 'Down girl. You've got real spirit, haven't you?'

Jess didn't appreciate his assessing of her character. She let her feet drop to the floor and stood up. 'I'm going to my room okay,' she said, and added, 'If that's all right with you?'

'You're always going to your room,' Ben said as she headed away.

Jess turned around to face him. 'Is that a crime?'

'No, but — oh forget it.' He shook his head dismissively. 'Good.'

Jess retreated to her room, feeling annoyed with him. She found it impossible to dislike Ben though. He was quiet and amiable. Several times he'd tried to strike up a conversation with her. Every time Jess managed to escape with a tactful reply or a physical departure. Ben could have taken her manner as a personal rejection and left her alone, but instead, kept trying to get through to her.

The next day was Friday, the second day of Jess's suspension. Erica was going to visit her sister across the other side of town. Jess had turned down an offer to go with her. If there was something she couldn't stand, it was sitting around listening to adults talk about the weather and people she didn't know. Before leaving, Erica put on the fridge a list of things Jess had to do before she returned. Jess studied the list — ironing, vacuuming, watering pot plants and loading the dishwasher. She didn't know where the iron was. She'd never used it. She looked first in the laundry, which seemed like the most logical place, but didn't find it. Maybe the kitchen, she thought doubtfully.

Jess began to go through the cupboards. She found piles of recipe books and dusty china — probably wedding presents never used. In the cupboard above the stove she came across the Bowman's liquor store. She let her eyes drift over the labels. She picked up a half full bottle of Irish Whiskey, and swivelled it around in her hand, examining the daunting contents. She remembered seeing many similar bottles littered around her parents' house, less than a year ago. Those bottles were always empty though. She replaced it carefully in its position in the cupboard.

Eventually Jess found the iron and ironing board in the hall cupboard and reluctantly set about the chores. She worked like a robot, moving mechanically through the tasks. At least it kept her busy, making the time go faster. Soon the others would be home from school, then a little later Erica would return. The house that was now empty and silent would be abuzz with chatter, laughter and talk of the weekend ahead. Jess didn't have any plans. Most of them had given up asking her along on their outings. She had given up making excuses.

When Jess returned to school things didn't run smoothly. She had found in Brianna a bitter enemy, who on her own return, went about turning against Jess anyone who would listen to her. She didn't have much trouble as she was popular and outspoken. Also, there was the Geography class. Ever since that first day, the ill-tempered teacher had taken a disliking to Jess. It was a feeling which extended both ways. Jess began frequenting the caravan park across the oval more often than she did the classroom. She started taking a change of clothes to school so as not to be recognised in her uniform on her trips beyond the school boundaries.

She thought it best not to skip every Geography class though, to avoid raising unnecessary suspicion. One afternoon as she strolled into the classroom she was jumped upon almost immediately by Mr Zelic.

'Where have you been for the last four lessons?' he demanded harshly.

Jess responded quickly. 'In the sick room.'

'Oh, I see. And are you a permanent invalid or is it just *my* lessons that make you sick?'

His cynical nature repulsed her.

'It's just a virus going around, I guess,' she mumbled, heading for her seat. She didn't want to create another storm. Mr Zelic was feeding off Jess's every word.

'Have you done the assignment then?' he said in a tone that implied he already anticipated the answer. Jess shook her head.

'No, well of course you haven't. Silly me for thinking you might have.'

Jess was managing to control herself. She sensed him trying to taunt her. So far, he had failed to evoke a response. Since Jess's arrival, the Year ten Geography class had experienced quite a bit of entertainment at her expense. She didn't like being the centre of attention, especially when she was the one being mocked.

'What would be a suitable punishment for our little truant here?' he mused out loud. The rest of the class had now assembled. He turned to face them.

'Do any of you young louts have any creative suggestions for some discipline for this young lady?' The class stared silently back at him. Jess was still standing at the front of the room, facing them. She dropped herself down into a chair. Mr Zelic turned instantly upon her.

'Did I say you could sit down? If I had my way, when I'd finished with you, you wouldn't be *able* to sit down. But they don't let us lay a hand on kids these days. Teachers have no authority anymore.'

Jess remained where she was.

'Did you hear what I said?' the teacher bellowed. Jess lifted her head. Everyone was watching her now, some with a faint glimmer of amusement on their faces, others simply inquisitive. How she despised those faces — every one of them.

'Girl, can't you obey a simple instruction?'

His rantings were being met with a blank response. It was

as though Jess was frozen to her seat, like a time bomb, waiting to explode. She did not explode.

'How do you think you went on the last test? Come on, have a guess,' he coaxed devilishly. He marched over to his desk and picked something up. He returned to the centre of the room, and as if making some sort of grand presentation, held up Jess's marked test paper. A large red encircled letter *E* adorned the page.

'This is what slackers get. It's good that we have someone like Jess in our class, it shows everyone what they don't want to be like.' He was clearly enjoying making an example of her. He slammed the paper down in front of Jess, causing her to jump. She raised her head to look up into his face. His beard quivered as he moved his teeth back and forth over each other. His eyes blazed with rage, and his ugly face seemed to glow with satisfaction over the discomfort he was causing her. Jess was suddenly filled with hatred.

'I know what your punishment shall be,' he announced, turning back to face the class, as if performing a recital to an audience.

'Stand up,' he demanded.

After a pause of a second or two, Jess rose slowly to her feet.

Mr Zelic pointed to the blackboard. 'You can write one hundred lines — *I must not continue to disgrace my school with my impertinence and foolishness.*' Jess hesitated for a moment, then without changing the expression on her face she turned towards the board. She could feel two dozen eyes drilling through her. With a shaking hand she picked up the chalk.

'Hurry up. You've wasted enough of the lesson as it is. These kids want to learn something, not sit here soaking up your wretched example.'

Jess began to spell out the humiliating words. The chalk scraped against the board. She pressed harder. It crumbled under the force she applied and sent a fine white powder cascading down the board where it collected on the ledge. Mr Zelic had turned his attention away from her and was lecturing to the class about an upcoming assignment. Jess felt like she was in a dream, barely aware of the sensation of her feet touching the floor. The words on the board seemed to scream at her. *Why was she doing this? Why was she allowing him to control her?* She could hear his voice, as if somewhere off in the distance. She heard the chalk she'd been holding drop to the floor. Slowly, she turned around. Her eyes flashed briefly from one side of the room to the other then stopped on the door. In one swift and silent movement she was over to it, and without looking back, she was gone.

Jess drew her key from her pocket. She knew of something that would take the anguish away. She'd learnt many things from her father. Once in the kitchen Jess paused for a moment. Her heart began to beat faster. Standing on her tip toes, she opened the cupboard above the stove. The doors flung back and hit the wood, making a loud clanking sound. She reached up and clutched her fingers around one of the bottles. Quickly she took it off the shelf and unscrewed the lid. She brought the top of the bottle up to her nose, and then pulled her head away from the pungent smell which made her eyes water.

In all her fourteen years Jess had never tasted alcohol. She'd had many chances, but she was afraid of it. When she was little she had thought that one sip would turn her into an uncontrollably violent person. Now after all those years of it being an enemy, it was about to become a comforter and a friend.

She put the bottle to her lips and tilted it upwards, taking a huge gulp. The potent liquid stung her throat as it went down. She screwed up her face and then broke into a fit of coughing. It was a strong spirit that she had chosen. She hadn't even bothered to read the label on the bottle.

When Jess awoke, she was covered by a blanket and it was dark all around her. She looked over at the window which was merely a blurred image. As she lay still, she tried to sort things out in her head. The memory of what she had done flashed through her mind. It was a thought almost as black as the darkness that surrounded her. Soon the silence and stillness became unbearable. She sat bolt upright. For a moment she felt like she was back on that park bench, the day she'd walked into the hospital. The feeling was similar, although it was a much stranger sensation.

Shakily, Jess rose to her feet. The room seemed to spin several times before she could take a step. She made her way into the hallway and inched along it to the bathroom. After several blind attempts she managed to flick the switch on the wall. The light stung her eyes, and the humming of the fluorescent globe in the socket sounded like a lawnmower at close range.

She looked in the mirror. What she saw was not her at all, but a dishevelled mess with the features of a human being. She hung her head. Even now, with the effects of the alcohol still gripping her, a feeling of remorse began creeping its way through her. Before returning to her room, she vomited into the wash basin. The part of her mind that was capable of conscious thought told her that she had never felt worse. She lay on the bed. Her body could not relax. Throughout the rest of the night, scenes of her life flashed before her — even things she wouldn't normally have remembered. But the nightmares were dominated by the events that had taken place since the night she'd run away from Wellingwood.

Jess slept late into the morning. When she woke, she didn't want to see anyone. She stayed concealed in her room, a prisoner of her own deeds. To think that she'd stooped as low as her father and John made her even more ashamed. If people didn't think she was irresponsible enough already, now they certainly would. Some of those people had told her that one day she would pay for acting without thinking about the consequences, but she had never really believed them. Now she was paying.

CHAPTER 14

Jess did not want to face the day. She did not want to face the rest of her life, or the people in it. Her bedroom seemed like the safest place to stay. The crowded, cheerful breakfast table held even less appeal than usual. She sat on the floor by her bed, half listening to the voices that came from the other rooms of the house. She could hear Ben's radio through the wall:

And today we're heading for another fine day with a glorious maximum of twenty-six degrees, so don't forget to hang out your washing before you head down to the beach for a day in the sun. But make sure you slap on that sun screen and ...

Washing! Beach! Jess realised that despite her misery, there were people in the world who welcomed the day ahead, and whose lives continued in their pleasurable monotony. Nevertheless, Jess thought she recognised something forced and robotic in the radio announcer's voice.

The house grew quiet. Jess wondered whether they had forgotten her, or maybe they just didn't care, or perhaps even hated her for what she had done. This thought in itself didn't bother her, but she knew that the behaviour of the family would be a constant reminder. The Bowmans had gone to school and work as normal, without even a thought for her. It was as though she didn't live there. It was as though she didn't even exist. Why did she bother to stay there? But would anywhere else be different?

Once she was sure she was alone in the house, she ventured out of her bedroom, and headed down the hall to the bathroom. As she splashed cold water over her face, she caught sight of another face in the mirror. Spinning around, she saw Robert's tall, wiry form standing in the doorway, leaning casually against the frame, like a cowboy against the bar in a western movie. She should have known they wouldn't leave her alone again. She pushed past him. He tried to stop her. As soon as she felt the pressure of his hand on her shoulder, she jerked quickly away. The doorframe hit her head, sending new shock waves through it. She glanced up at Robert's alarmed face, then ran down the hall and back into her room. Robert followed. As he entered the room, Jess was already lying on her bed, eyes closed, as if in some kind of instantaneous sleep. He walked over to her. Jess's eyes fluttered open to see him standing there, looking down at her. She let her eyes drop shut again, without acknowledging his presence, hoping that if she ignored him long enough he would go away. He didn't. She heard his voice, quiet and gentle.

'Jess.' He waited a few seconds then repeated her name. 'Jess.'

Her eyes reluctantly flickered open again.

'How're you feeling?' His manner was patient and quite calm. Jess had never heard him raise his voice to any of his children. His tactics were always more subtle, and they usually seemed to get results.

She tried to shrug her shoulders.

'Jess, why did you have to go and do such a thing? Why?'
She would not speak to him.

'Is it us? Is it something we've done? Please, you have to tell me.'

'It's not you,' Jess squeaked. Her answer was not altogether truthful.

'What then? I don't understand.' Robert's voice sounded intense and desperate.

'That's right. You *don't* understand. You just have no idea about me, or my life or anything!' Her silence was broken, and she sat up and exploded into a fit of anger. 'You don't know me at all. You think you do but you don't. You think that because all your other kids are perfect, *I* have to be as well. You expect me to just come here and like it and be best friends with everybody. You just expect me to forget what has happened in my life and to act like you're my personal saviour. Well I can't forget everything just like that. There was only one thing that would let me forget.' She collapsed into a barrage of sobs. As soon as she'd said this last sentence she regretted it. Now he probably thought she was an alcoholic, but she didn't care. Robert looked stunned.

'Jess,' he said, but he couldn't think of anything else to say. He stood silently. The corners of his mouth twitched slightly, betraying a degree of helplessness.

'Please, just leave me alone,' Jess pleaded.

'I can't do that. You need our help.'

'You can't say or do anything that will help.' She wanted

to be rid of his intrusion. Robert looked hurt. He looked at her defiant face that had now reverted to staring blankly up at the ceiling, eyes fixed and burning with years of unreleased emotion. With a shake of his head, he granted her wish and returned her world to solitude once again.

The closed room became stuffy. The light emanating from the globe on the ceiling became glaring and unpleasant. She didn't have the strength to get up and switch it off. All day Jess lay there, locked in her cage of self-pity. She heard the other kids come home from school, turn on the TV, and open and close the fridge for what seemed like a million times. She heard Erica's voice. It had become very familiar to her. She always seemed to be saying something to the other kids. To Erica, the pandemonium of the household was a comforting symbol of a Healthy family life, but to Jess it was an unbearable reminder of the ease with which other people carried on with their daily lives.

Jess found herself thinking of Serena, the painfully normal girl whose life seemed to radiate satisfaction. She wondered what Serena's life had been like before she'd come to live with the Bowmans. Her mind conjured up a picture of a drunken father and a crowd of grubby children competing for the last slice of bread in a tumble-down shack. Somehow the picture didn't fit. Perhaps she had run away from home, from rich parents who had stopped granting their spoilt child's every wish. She wondered if Serena had to live on the streets, whether she was ever almost raped or so hungry she had to steal her food. Jess doubted it.

Her reflective thoughts were interrupted by a knock on the door. After hearing the knock again, she called out, 'Who is it?'

'It's me,' Erica's voice sang out, muffled through the timber. Jess was relieved it wasn't Robert or Ben.

'Come in,' she murmured reluctantly, readying herself for an earful.

Erica entered the room, carrying a sandwich on a plate. She set it down on the bedside table. Jess tossed a glance at it. She didn't feel in the mood for meatloaf.

'Have something to eat,' Erica said, sounding sympathetic. Jess shook her head. Erica sat on the edge of the bed.

'I know you probably feel bad right now, but you can't stay in here for the rest of your life.'

Jess didn't reply but waited to see what else she would say.

'Jess if you have a problem with alcohol, we can get you some help.'

Jess felt like screaming out that it wasn't alcohol that terrorised her. If only it were that simple.

'There are ways to deal with things like this and staying in your room is not one of them.'

A pause followed.

'Won't you at least talk to us about what's worrying you?' Another pause. 'We don't expect you to be perfect. The other kids aren't perfect either. But you're not them, you're Jessica Dimitri, an individual person, with individual needs. We'd like to help you meet those needs.'

Jess thought the words sounded worn and rehearsed. Nothing she'd heard so far was in the least bit comforting.

'We love you for who you are. It's got nothing to do with the crazy things you might do.'

Love! What was that?

'So, I'm crazy, am I?'

'No, not crazy. I didn't mean to say crazy … I meant disturbed — no, irrational.'

Jess thought she could sense the composed, assured exterior begin to fall away.

'Please, Jess, please come out and cheer up. You've got to stop feeling so sorry for yourself like this.' Now she sounded impatient. Jess didn't know what to do or say. She felt uncomfortable with Erica's imploring words — *'You've got to stop feeling so sorry for yourself.'*

Eventually Erica gave up and left her with the meatloaf. Jess had triumphed once again. She had not been intimidated or influenced by the words. That was what counted. Regardless of what else happened, she knew that she could go on, as long as she kept her independence. After the roller coaster ride of the last few weeks, she was still her own person — that at least, was a comforting thought.

The rain drops beat rhythmically against the car window. Jess watched each one roll down the glass and sink into a pool of anonymity. She could not believe where they were taking her. All her reassuring confidence in herself and her independence, it seemed, had been in vain. The control she'd felt in her bedroom had vanished. When Robert and Erica had told her that they were taking her to see a psychologist,

Jess's first reaction was disbelief, followed by anger and a feeling of betrayal. The shock had weakened her defence, and her frail objections were not enough to prevent the dreaded from happening.

Jess managed to hang onto some sort of mental composure until the car pulled into the car park. Then she began to panic. She looked at the large old stone building of the clinic. What was going to happen? Nobody spoke until they reached the door.

'I hope this guy's good,' Robert said quietly under his breath as they stood briefly before the door, looking at the small neat plaque secured to it: *J.B. McInnen Ph.D (Psych)*. Erica put a hand on Jess's shoulder. She tossed it aside roughly and hurried inside, simply to increase the distance between her and the Bowmans. The receptionist glanced up and smiled at Jess. She was young — very young, perhaps only a few years older than Jess. She watched Jess take a seat in the corner furthest from the desk. When Jess's eyes met hers again the smile reappeared, then she looked away and seemed to be pretending to fill out some appointment cards. Erica sat next to Jess and Robert went over to the baby-faced receptionist and said something quietly to her, then took up a seat next to his wife.

The waiting room was dimly lit — even in comparison to the bleak skies outside. From somewhere drifted the sound of soft classical music. It all seemed to be trying to create an artificial ambience. The furnishings reflected the doctor's success. Jess had never seen anything like it. The walls were a red wood panelling with the skirting boards painted gold. An intricate gold pattern ran along the edges of the walls and ceiling. The chairs they sat on were an ebony-looking wood made in an antique style. Oversized reproductions of paintings by Renoir, Monet and other impressionist artists, all in elaborate frames, hung on the walls. Jess's anger was momentarily subdued by the awe of her surroundings. She almost laughed aloud when she saw the hourly fees on a small noticeboard by the reception desk. Were Robert and Erica really paying that much for her to see a useless shrink? She suddenly felt victorious again.

Just then, the door to the inner office opened, and a thin middle-aged man with red hair and a short clipped beard came out. He was followed by another man, who in contrast, had black hair, was clean shaven, and wore casual trousers and a shirt which Jess thought much too bright and cheerful for a psychologist to be wearing. When the first man saw them, he looked self-conscious and hurried over to the reception desk. Jess wondered what was wrong with this man's head — he looked normal enough to her.

The doctor introduced himself, shook hands with Erica and Robert and put out his hand for Jess, who pretended she didn't see it. Dr McInnen, looking totally unfazed, ushered Jess into his office.

'Ah — we'd better come in too I think,' Robert said hurriedly, clearly trying not to be intimidated by this man.

Jess found herself in an even grander looking room. She looked around for the couch, but there wasn't one. He told her to sit in a chair already positioned in front of a desk and directed Erica and Robert to sit on either side. The panic had now returned.

'And what can I do for you?' he asked, probably for the umpteenth time that day. He was looking at Jess, but she didn't know it, her eyes were glued to the carpet.

'We think Jess would benefit from some counselling,' Robert offered. She's having a hard time at school. Perhaps she can tell you about it.' They waited for a response from Jess, but none came. Robert continued, in a slightly less sympathetic manner. 'She's very hostile toward us and she doesn't mix with anybody. In fact, we have a hard time getting her to come out of her room. She only does what she has to do, sometimes not even that.'

'Right, well—'

'She's almost constantly in some sort of strife at school. She won't talk to us about any of it.' His verbalising of Jess's faults angered her. She managed to remain calm. She opened her mouth to say something but stopped herself. She was not going to give them any ammunition. A new plan was formulating in her mind. To get her revenge on the Bowmans for bringing her here would simply require doing the opposite to everything they expected. She would be polite, even amiable. She would make them all look like such fools. It would be easy. The thought was so inviting that Jess had to stop herself from allowing a smile to cross her lips. She realised the doctor was talking to her.

'So, Jess, would you like to start by telling me some of the things that are bothering you?'

What was she supposed to say to that? Where could she possibly begin? Jess's mind was ticking over. He waited for a reply. When he didn't receive one he addressed her again.

'And how are you feeling right now?'

What kind of question was that? She shifted uneasily in her seat, her skin squeaking against the leather. How did she feel? Did she know? Robert and Erica seemed as uncomfortable in the silence as Jess did, but the psychologist continued.

'Is there something that you're afraid of?'

Why did he have to ask questions like this? How could she put her plan into action if he kept asking her such absurd questions?

'Answer the questions,' Robert said through his teeth. Jess could sense that his usual serene, unaffected demeanour was teetering. She lifted her head to look the doctor in the eye. He was leaning forward in his grandly upholstered seat, his hands folded calmly in his lap. It was almost as though he was trying to stare her out. She looked away towards the window. The dark clouds moving across the sombre sky were all that was visible through it. Jess didn't like the pattern on the curtains — it was a bizarre spiralling design. She looked away from it. It was probably supposed to draw her into a trance — hypnotise her, so she would do what they wanted. She wouldn't look at those curtains again for the entire time she was there. She was determined not to let this man work any of his magic on her.

'And what about school, how do you feel about that? Do you have any friends that you talk to?'

At last, an easier question. She could tell him that she had lots of friends and was happy going to school. Couldn't she? Yes of course, it was easy. Wasn't it? Why couldn't she tell him she had lots of friends? The silence was painful.

The doctor remained calm and continued. 'And what is it about school you don't like?' He seemed sure he'd get a response for this assumption. He was wrong.

Out of the corner of her eye, Jess could see Robert's foot tapping rhythmically and seemingly unconsciously against the floor. Erica was sitting straight and tense, her handbag clasped in her lap. Her fingernails dug into the vinyl and her knuckles were white.

'And how do you get along with the teachers at your school?'

Jess hated the way he began his sentences with '*And*'. It annoyed her intensely, as did his calm demeanour.

The barrage of questions continued, as if searching for something that would trick her into responding. Still there was silence. She stared at the floral design on the rug. She could feel them watching her, just as on that first day at Stonewell High School. She shuddered as she remembered.

After about half an hour of the one-sided conversation, J. B. McInnen straightened up and gave an assessment.

'I think your behaviour probably stems from some deep psychological scarring sustained in early life, causing you to retreat and withdraw from anything that makes you feel uncomfortable. This seems likely to me, given your background. You probably possess a phobia, or even several, that prevents you from showing normal social behaviour. It seems like you feel unloved and as though everyone's against you, although of course this fear is a false fear. Your head is playing tricks on you. There is also the possibility of a personality disorder.'

Jess couldn't believe it. He was talking about her as if she was a laboratory rat in an experiment — as if she wasn't even there. She knew she was not a person to him. She was simply another client whose money fed his family and furnished his house. Jess suddenly felt a bitter hatred for this calm, patient man. She watched him for several more seconds then rose to her feet.

'You can all go to hell,' she said in a low shaky voice.

She flicked a glance at each of the three faces, then ran from the office and through the waiting room. The receptionist looked up in surprise as Jess hurtled towards the door. She ran across the car park. It had begun to rain again. She stopped for a moment, breathing hard, and looked around for somewhere to go. She heard Robert's voice, loud and angry behind her. Immediately she began to run again, but only got as far as the other side of the car park. He was upon her. Jess twisted and struggled, but it was impossible to move. Robert held her wrists firmly above her head. He held her against a parked car. The pain shot through her arms as she wrenched them back and forth.

'Let me *go*!' she screamed viciously, flinging her body from side to side, desperate to free herself. An unknown terror gripped her. In Robert's grasp she felt a wave of panic.

She felt sick. All her instincts told her to fight, to get away from him. It was as if her life depended on it. Her face was drenched with sweat and rain. She was like a wild animal, fighting for survival.

Jess felt herself being dragged away from the slippery metal of the car, and then thrown across the back seat of the Bowman's car. She had been defeated. Digging her fingers into the seat, as if it was a person's skin, seemed to direct some of the anger away from her body. She bit the dusty fabric of the seat cover. It tasted like an old sock. The car swung out of the car park with its miserable load, and headed west, away from the big old building.

CHAPTER 15

Jess's fight hadn't been exhausted. She sat hunched on the back seat of the car, waiting for her next opportunity. It came as the car came to a halt at an intersection. Quickly, she slid her fingers under the door latch. In a swift movement she flung open the door and slipped outside. Once again, she ran, not pausing to look back. She had been running for so long now, from people, from places. She wove her way between the stationary vehicles and ducked down a side street. She knew they couldn't follow her this time, the car was immobilised between two others. She was the victor after all.

As her breath came back to her and the dizziness disappeared, she noticed her surroundings for the first time. It was a part of town she'd never seen. Tall brick houses, close together, almost touching in places, lined the foot path on both sides. The houses all looked the same, apart from the positioning of the pot plants. They all had a window either side of the centred front door. The arrangement seemed to create a face, which looked at her curiously and seemed to be sympathising with her.

Jess felt her muscles ache as she let them relax, and the tension ebbed away. She wiped her brow with her sleeve. The air was still damp and cool. She sloshed through puddles in the gutter like a small child. The next street along ran diagonally toward the main road. Jess followed it dazedly, feeling better now that she was free again. She came to the corner and rounded it. As she did so, her heart sank. The sight of the Bowman's pale blue station wagon hit her in the face like a fist. She turned impulsively toward the nearest public building and quickly stepped inside. It took her a moment to realise that she'd just entered the police station. Robert stood at the counter, talking to the officer behind it. When he saw her a look of astonishment crossed his face.

'Nice of you to drop in,' he said. Jess stood still on the spot, feeling strangely calm.

'I'm not going home with you,' she said matter-of-factly, after a few moments in which nobody spoke.

'You can't spend your whole life running away from things, you know.'

'If you had to take the shit that I have to, you wouldn't want to go home with you either.' Jess looked at the officer. This was her chance to get back at Robert. It had the desired effect. The policeman shot a sharp look in Robert's direction, but didn't say anything.

'You've got a nerve, saying something like that after your behaviour recently.'

'There are laws against men who molest girls,' Jess dared. Robert looked at her, puzzled.

'What are you talking about?'

Jess knew that what she was doing could get Robert into serious trouble, *but whatever it takes*, she thought ruthlessly. Her priority, as it had been most of her life, was to look after herself. 'The other night, after everyone had gone to bed, he came into my room and tried to touch me.'

'She's lying,' Robert said, looking desperately at the officer.

Jess narrowed her eyes. 'You've never been able to keep your hands to yourself.'

'Why are you saying these things, you know they're not true?'

'Hang on a minute. What's the actual problem here?' the confused officer asked.

'I'm not going home with him,' Jess repeated with greater conviction and a backward toss of her head.

'You will do what you're told.'

'I don't have to do anything, you're not my father.'

Now the policeman was completely confused. He had been joined by a younger looking officer.

'These are serious allegations, Sir,' he said, looking at Robert.

'Why do they always believe the kid?' Robert barked. 'She's lying. The girl is lying!'

Jess stood watching the three men and the unfolding scene.

'You realise we have to investigate claims of this nature?'

'This is ridiculous. Jess is my responsibility. I've never done anything to her. She's coming home with me.' He stalked over to Jess and grabbed her by the arm.

'You can't make me.'

'She's right, you know,' the younger officer said. 'Under such circumstances the child has the right to a suspended custody until an investigation can be carried out.'

'I don't believe this,' Robert said. 'You try to do the right thing by them and they go and knife you in the back. Tell me where she's going to go then.'

'Are there some friends you can stay with?'

Jess shook her head.

'To a refuge then, I suppose,' was the quick reply.

'No way!' Jess cried, equally quickly.

'I'm sorry, but that's your alternative.'

The thought conjured up images of Wellingwood.

'I'd rather die,' she said indignantly.

'Then maybe you'd like it in there,' one of the officers smirked, flinging open a door to reveal the bars of a cell, set back from the office. Jess's face turned pale. Surely, he was joking. Jess sensed Robert now gaining the upper hand.

'Sure, I don't care,' she said, her pride swelling. She looked at her three oppressors with an expression as if to say, 'I can handle anything you throw at me.'

The policeman who had made the offer hesitated, then realising that he now had little choice but to lock her up, said, 'Very well. If that's what you want. But you can only stay here until the morning, until something can be worked out.'

After several more minutes discussion Jess's fate was sealed. She would spend the night in the police station and the next day a case would be filed, pending investigation, against Robert Bowman for indecent assault. Robert left the station, seemingly in a state of complete shock, muttering something about parents' rights and the state of the law. Jess was led to the back of the station, a little in shock herself, at the events that had just taken place. She spent an hour or so in one of the interview rooms, before being taken to the cell and told it was almost time to close the station for the night. There would be a single officer on duty if she needed anything.

Once in her new dwellings, she began inspecting the surroundings. She was relieved that she didn't have to face the Bowmans that night. They couldn't get her here. No one could. She was safe. She looked around the cell. It was quite large. The walls were painted a dull pea green, possibly symbolic of the envy the inhabitants most likely felt for those on the other side of the bars. Jess was not envious. She was glad there was no one to bother her. The floor was a kind of paved lino. A single light globe dangled from the ceiling. There was a small door in the far corner. Jess went over to check out the conveniences. There was a small metal toilet, not unlike the ones found in trains. She lifted the lid. It was clean and even smelled hygienic. The roll of paper was half empty and was yellowing slightly. Jess marvelled that she might be using toilet paper from the same roll as a bank robber, or even a murderer. She imagined to herself what kind of offender last occupied these quarters. She turned on a tap. No hot water.

Jess looked around and wondered where she was supposed to sleep. There was a wooden bench along one wall. She sat down on it. From where she was she could see into the front of the station, through the door which had been left half open. A flicker of light, reflected off the glass outside door, ran briefly across the floor, indicating that it had been opened. A woman walked in and stood at the counter. She was directly in Jess's line of sight. After a moment or two, the woman's eyes met Jess's, and lingered for several seconds on the unlikely looking prisoner. Jess wondered what she was thinking. A second later, a blue-sleeved arm reached across and pulled the door shut, so that her view was extinguished. Jess could hear the police officer talking to the woman for several moments, then there was silence. Now Jess was completely in solitude. She felt like a criminal.

As the time ticked by she became slightly restless, pacing the cell like an anxious animal in a cage. When her legs grew tired, she lay down on the wooden bench. It was so narrow that she had to keep one hand on the floor to prevent herself toppling off. In this close vicinity to the wall Jess discovered several patches of tiny writing, obviously scribed by past inmates. Some of it was written in blue ball point pen, and some in red. Jess strained her eyes to read it. The words were a legacy of the bitter feelings of newly captured criminals and outlined explicitly what they'd thought of their captors, in very colourful language.

A while later, a policeman came through the door, wheeling a folding camp bed and mattress.

'We don't usually have people in here over night. Usually send 'em to the city. You'll have to make do with this.' He was not the same man who had brought her to the cell. She decided that the shifts must have changed. He was tall and very thin, and also very young. He had short dark hair, dark eyes and an olive complexion like Jess's own. The movement of his lips as he spoke accentuated dimples in both his cheeks.

He was 'succulent', in Olivia's terms. 'I'm afraid we're going to have to keep you locked in here — regulations.' He didn't look Jess in the eye as he spoke.

'How am I supposed to have a shower?' she asked, more to test him than out of genuine desire for such a convenience.

'You should have thought of that before you turned down the refuge.' The constable was brief and to the point.

'Do you often have people in here like this?' She asked.

'No, not often.'

'Do I get anything to eat, or do I have to starve as well?'

He looked at her disapprovingly, misreading her cynicism for hostility.

'Constable Livingstone will bring you something later,' he said. 'Now be good and don't get too comfortable. We don't want you recommending the accommodation to your friends.' He smiled to himself at his own humour as he locked the cell and left the station.

For the next fifteen minutes Jess tried to negotiate the folding bed. It was old, and when she finally had it set up so that the objecting legs didn't give way with her weight, a cloud of dust was circulating around the cell. The blankets and pillow she'd been provided with were cleaner, and she was able to form a satisfactory sleeping surface. She lay down carefully on the mattress. The low bed sunk almost to the floor. Jess heard footsteps in the front of the station, and one of the officers from earlier appeared, carrying a Styrofoam fast food container.

'I hope you like burgers,' he said to her, handing it through the bars. Jess shrugged her shoulders. He brought her some water in a paper cup, and while she drank he explained what would happen in the morning. The procedure seemed complicated and needless to Jess. She was fast beginning to realise that the process would most likely be long and messy, and she'd probably have to go to court if she was going to press charges against Robert. Jess was not really listening to the rest of what he said, but simply nodded from time to time.

He finally left her to her dinner. She heard him flick several switches, including some of the lights in the front of the building, gearing down for the night. There was a dim light in the corridor, which she was told would be switched off in half an hour.

Jess sat on the bed and inspected her meal. It was greasy and unappetising. The mayonnaise had already begun to run out into the bottom of the container. But she hadn't eaten much in two days, so once she began to eat, she did so ravenously.

After the light had gone out, she was in total darkness except for the glow from the front reception area and a glimmer of a street light, cast on the floor at the front of the station through the glass doors. There was an occasional extra flicker of light as a car drove along the street outside. Jess lay on her back on the bed, staring up at the blackness of the ceiling. She could hear the clock ticking rhythmically in the office, and the wind swirling about ferociously outside. Occasionally, a dog would bark in the distance. The sounds compounded the feeling of isolation. In the darkness, all modern and comforting aspects of her surroundings seemed to vanish. She felt like she was in a dungeon in a castle in medieval times. The dripping of the tap in the bathroom alcove fell into step with the ticking of the clock and contributed further to the sensation.

Jess couldn't sleep. She didn't want to sleep. She sat with her legs hugged tightly to her chest. Dark thoughts of the day began to creep into her mind. The last incident at school she'd tried so hard to forget was a life-like picture in her mind. It was followed by the desperate pursuit of oblivion and the consequent shame she'd felt. She tried to shrug all thoughts away but found it impossible to empty her mind.

The accusations she'd made against Robert, stayed with her, almost haunted her. Had she gone too far this time? What would happen now? This had always been the question — the question of uncertainty. What had she achieved that day? Revenge? Freedom from the Bowmans? They would all be talking about her, their evil foster daughter. *Screw them*, she thought. They could all go to hell. Hell was where it felt like she was, only it was cold.

As the night wore on, the temperature dropped still further, as all the daytime heat diffused to the outside world. Still Jess sat on top of her blankets. Pictures of John and Margi and Margi's ever-present strained expression came to her ... then the letter that she'd torn up and thrown away was suddenly pieced back together like a jigsaw puzzle. She found herself reading the bold black words over and over again. Her thoughts ran in a sort of backwards sequence. The dark graveyard that matched the darkness of the cell. Her flight from Olivia's room and Olivia's spiteful face.

The darkness continued. This time it was filled by a man with a bullet around his neck and the glare of headlights. The sweat began to trickle down Jess's forehead as she relived the terror of that night. Her renewed anger for Zac reached a crescendo so that she almost screamed out loud. Jess found herself thinking of all the men she'd ever known — her father, John, Robert, her dead brother and Travis. Travis could hardly qualify as a man, but he fitted into the same hateful category as the rest of those who'd abused her.

Thoughts of her brother flowed into her mind for the first time in weeks. Maybe if he hadn't have died, things would have been different. He had been far from the perfect sibling, but he always seemed to be close by in her times of greatest need. The one person with whom she'd shared even the weakest of bonds had been cruelly wrenched away. The world hated her, and she hated it back.

Jess sat in her cage, shivering from the cold against her bare skin and not conscious enough to think of getting under the blankets, but able to be aware of the turmoil inside her head. The minutes ticked by, as slowly as earthly possible. She was waiting for a morning that would perhaps never come, and maybe the world would be shrouded in lonely darkness forever, or at least the part of the world where Jess was. She felt like a frightened child waking from a nightmare which had seemed so real. But it was worse, because it *was* real.

CHAPTER 16

Morning did come, and Jess knew what she was going to do. The bed had eventually been used but hadn't provoked sleep or eased her mind. She waited for someone to come. She had no idea what the time was. The wind had died down and the sound of early morning bird song was clear even through the thick walls of the cell. Jess had begun to feel claustrophobic, despite two of the walls consisting only of bars. One night in this place was definitely enough. The refuge didn't seem as unappealing as it had the night before. Now though, she wouldn't need it.

As soon as the junior Constable arrived, he went to Jess's cell. Immediately, she demanded to be let out, and proceeded to tell him, without any accompanying emotion, that she no longer wished to press charges against Robert. She asked that he call the Bowmans and tell them to come and pick her up.

'What's the reason for this sudden turn around?' he asked.

'I lied,' Jess said unemotionally.

He looked at her gravely. 'Why would you do that?'

Jess shrugged her shoulders but wouldn't give an explanation.

'That's a serious thing to accuse someone of,' he chided. Jess shrugged again but didn't speak.

'Anyway, because of the nature of your claims we may still need to investigate.'

Jess's heart sunk again. Things were just getting too complicated. 'You'll still let me go home with them though, won't you?'

'For now I guess you can, but I can assure you we'll be keeping an eye on things.'

Jess's decision had been an agonising one, and only slightly influenced by any guilt she felt, rather, to save herself any trauma even remotely resembling that of her last two breaks between homes. At least she knew the Bowmans. It wasn't as if she had to talk to them or pretend to like them. No one could force her to do that.

The previous night had changed her perspective. She couldn't win. No matter what she did she was trapped. This way she would at least know what she was in for. Jess knew that she would only be playing to the tune of the vicious circle that controlled her life if she shunned the Bowmans. She was cornered whichever way she looked at it. Jess knew it would be even harder to live in the house with the rest of them now. She had cursed herself with her own actions yet again.

It was Erica who pulled up outside the station. Jess was thankful for this and wondered whether the reason for it was significant. She spoke briefly to the officer before turning to Jess, as though forced to. She didn't smile, but ushered Jess towards the door. To Jess's surprise, Erica didn't speak to her. She drove as if the passenger seat beside her was empty, which was a reception Jess hadn't anticipated. When she'd been suspended from school or been drunk, Erica had never shown anything but sympathy and support. Now she was cold, not even offering a greeting in the station. Jess wondered whether she'd made the right decision after all.

The weather was still inclement. Spits of rain were being wiped away methodically by the windscreen wipers which squeaked menacingly on each downward stroke. After the tedious night in the station the noise was unbearably repetitive, and Jess couldn't stand it any longer. She forced herself to speak to break up the monotony.

'I suppose you think I'm the scum of the earth after yesterday.' To discuss any other subject would have been out of the question.

'What you said about Robert was virtually unforgivable, but we're not in the business of turning our back on a person who we've made a commitment to help.' Erica's eyes remained fixed unswervingly on the wet road ahead. 'I don't suppose you know what it's like to take a complete stranger into your home and attempt to pick up the pieces of a broken life.' Jess thought of several cynical replies but held them back. She didn't want to get into an argument. Instead she let Erica continue. She was in full swing now.

'We knew it was a gamble taking in a teenager from God knows where. We knew that. We've done it before.'

'And Serena came out smelling like roses and you expect me to as well. I'm sorry but I'm going to have to disappoint you.'

'It doesn't work like that. You are not Serena, you are Jess.'

Jess had heard this line of argument before. She wondered whether it was a standard line all parents used.

'We have no expectations except that you live by our simple, reasonable rules. If Serena can do that, so can you.'

'But it's easy for her. It's *always* been easy for her. *Life* is easy for her.'

'You don't know what she's been through. I know you think you've had the toughest deal of anyone on this earth, but I can assure you that you wouldn't want to have been in Serena's shoes a few years ago.' Erica's deliberate undermining of Jess's suffering angered her.

Erica hesitated then went on. 'Your foster sister was born in New Zealand to a single teenage mother and given up at birth. She was adopted by the CEO of a multi-national company, but after he and his wife were killed in a car accident, she had a long succession of guardians and was eventually adopted again by a young couple with no other children. When the woman died of cancer, Serena became the victim of sexual abuse by her adoptive father. For about four years that went on, until, when she was twelve years old she realised there was something she could do about it. She told one of her teachers at school, and when her father found out he tried to kill her. He stabbed her with a kitchen knife, poor thing. It's a miracle she survived — a miracle.'

Jess sat in stunned silence. She didn't know whether to believe what she was hearing. It all sounded so inconceivable and contrived. Serena seemed so normal and care-free. Was

Erica trying to shock her into following Serena's example? For the rest of the journey they both sat in silence, Erica concentrating intensely on her driving, and Jess turning over in her mind what she'd just heard.

There was no one in sight when they arrived home. Jess wondered whether it had been planned that way to avoid her. Without another word to Erica she went to her room. It seemed like a long time since she'd been in there. The night had been an eternity in itself. The room was exactly as she'd left it — dirty clothes draped over the chair, curtains half closed, school bag tossed in a corner, not touched since her last vigil to school.

She stood just inside the door, surveying the room which had become a haven to her. Its familiarity was as loathsome as the rest of the world that surrounded her. For a moment her breath was short and shallow, like a drum roll, building up to a climax. With a sudden burst of ferocity, she grabbed a hair brush from the bedside table and hurled it as hard as she could across the room. It struck the mirror of her dresser and produced a large star-shaped crack in the glass. The essence of destruction about its appearance seemed to yank at something inside of her. With a rush of adrenaline, she leapt into motion, systematically treating with brutality any loose object in sight.

She emptied her school bag onto the floor. A cascade of pens and pencils flowed from it. She kicked at them viciously and they flew like missiles around the room. She ripped the drawers from the chest and emptied their contents across the room. She did the same with the wardrobe. The shoes gave her particular satisfaction, as they hit the wall with a loud hollow thump, often leaving a streak of shoe polish or dirt.

When she'd finished she began on the bed, tearing off the quilt and then the sheets. She grabbed the pillow and swiped at anything that remained in any sort of order. With a final rush of energy, she upturned the flimsy metal bed base. It landed on the piles of debris with a crash and a complaining squeak.

Jess stood still again, breathing heavily, as though she'd just run a marathon. In a way, she had. She looked at her trail of destruction — books bent and torn; pieces of glass or china that were once vases or ornaments littered the carpet. Tears stung her eyes. She couldn't bear to look at it any longer. She tripped her way out of the room and rushed down the hall.

The bathroom was the only place where she was sure to be alone. Standing in front of the mirror, Jess looked at the picture of her forlorn form. It seemed ghost-like and almost transparent to her eyes, which were wild with fire. The sleek eyebrows lowered over a brown shapely face — trembling lips — raven hair tossed about over her face as if at the mercy of a violent wind. She was a wreck, but it didn't matter — the contorted image was merely the body that bore her soul.

One of the sliding doors of the medicine cabinet was ajar. She swayed closer to it. A row of bottles stood out. Automatically, her eyes scanned the labels — aspirin, cough syrup, various stomach remedies, and some tablets Erica used to help her sleep. Jess vaguely remembered seeing something like it in the Pullin's bathroom. They were Margi's relief from a violent husband. Jess knew those pills were powerful. An overdose could surely be fatal. She reached into the cupboard, remembering what she'd said to Jack that night in the cemetery — *'It seems as though you have to be dead before you're appreciated.'* It seemed like a lifetime ago. She withdrew the bottle with a shaking hand and turned the lid slowly. As she did so, it slipped from her fingers and fell to the floor, shattering on the tiles. Jess stared at the fragments of glass and tiny white pills lying on the floor and over her feet.

She ran from the bathroom and back to the only place she knew where to go, the devastated scene of her bedroom. She sank lifelessly onto the carpet of broken memories and possessions. Now the tears began to flow — months' worth of captive tears. She sobbed loudly and uncontrollably into the uncomforting musty carpet, the bitterness finally releasing itself in a barrage of emotion.

* * *

The street light on the corner was beginning to take effect. There were no vehicles in sight. In the twilight, the sky was a luminescent dome above the tranquillity of the town. It was a cool evening. The slight wind nipped at Jess's bare legs as she stood there. The peaceful setting seemed to denounce any form of human tragedy.

She began to walk along the footpath. Being in the house

had become unbearable, with the others inquisitively aware of Jess's plight. The atmosphere was painful and the setting all too familiar. It didn't matter where she went, as long as it was away. The town was still largely alien to her. She followed the route she took to school, seeing many things she'd never really noticed before. Houses as foreign to her as if she'd never seen them were on either side. There was a vacant block grazing some sheep, an old billboard, and the church. The Stonewell Uniting Church was an historic stone building. Its steps led directly from the footpath to the door. Jess stopped to gaze up at it.

Her curiosity beckoned Jess forward toward the steps. She'd never been inside a church before. Carefully, she turned the door handle, as if it would break off in her hand. She didn't expect the door to be open, but it shifted easily with the slight pressure she applied. Jess hesitated, not really wanting to go in, but her sense of adventure was too great. She slipped inside and found herself in a tiny foyer. Jess quickly looked around to see if anyone was there and listened for any sign of movement. There was perfect silence. It reminded her of the silence of the prison cell.

On one side of her stood a table, with a lace cloth covering it, and books in several neat piles. Everything seemed so perfectly placed, so fastidiously arranged that Jess felt decidedly out of place. She tiptoed her way through to the body of the church, feeling like an intruder. She didn't know whether she was once again doing the wrong thing, whether she was entering into forbidden territory. Nevertheless, she continued down the aisle, not really knowing why she was tiptoeing, but feeling compelled to do so. It seemed important that she should not break the silence.

Through a high stained-glass window filtered a beam of light, perhaps from a street light, the setting sun or early moon. It fell in a soft array of colours on the varnished wooden seats. Jess found herself holding her breath as she cast her eyes over the ornaments at the front of the church — the spotless white altar cloth, the silver candle sticks, the tall cross with a man hanging on it. Jess's eyes came to a halt on a porcelain figure of the Virgin Mary, coloured softly and innocently. Jess knew what it was. It made her think of her own virginity. When she was in early high school a neighbourhood boy had asked her to go with him behind the bike shed. Jess had refused, knowing what probably would have happened. Later she'd thought about it and wished that maybe she had. Sex was not something she thought about a lot. It was as frightening to Jess as violence to a child, and the night she was attacked while hitch-hiking had heightened her fear. She was glad it was not something she had to deal with at the moment.

She stood at the front of the church a while longer. A kind of mystical power seemed to hang in the air. Jess didn't know whether she'd imagined it, but it seemed to be telling her she was neither welcome nor worthy to be there. She wondered whether there were such things as ghosts and spirits, and felt for certain now that there were.

After retreating from the haunting interior of the church,

Jess continued along the road, vowing never to go back. Almost before she realised it, she had reached the boundary of the school grounds. A school always looked so different when deserted. It reminded her of the Nazi concentration camps she'd seen in books, abandoned after the war. Jess didn't want to walk past the buildings. They were a symbol of the world's conspiracy against her.

She turned down the quiet street which led along the boundary fence of the oval, and towards the caravan park, which was a kinder sight. Between the park and the end of the school grounds was a cluster of trees, and a wooden bench where some of the kids assembled for a smoke at lunch time. It was a comfortable spot far away from the probing eyes of the teachers and was keenly contested for each school day. Jess sat down on the bench. She now had it all to herself.

She took a deep breath and let it out slowly and purposefully, letting her eyes drift across the wide expanse of green in front of her. Then they came to a stop. Not far from her stood a figure. Jess strained her eyes in the growing darkness to see. It soon became apparent that it was a boy about her age. As she watched, she recognised him from her class at school. It was Mark Traicos. He was kicking a football around on the grass, oblivious to Jess's presence. He fooled around, pretending to take a mark, kicked the goal, then raised his arms in triumph, as if to a crowd of spectators. He was muttering some self-commentary that Jess couldn't understand from where she was. A small amused smirk of a smile appeared at the corners of her lips.

Jess felt her stomach do a queer little flip. Perhaps it was empty, she was hungry. Her eyes still stung from crying. She watched Mark prancing around the field. Suddenly it seemed desperately important that he shouldn't see her. When his back was turned, Jess slipped through the trees and instead of going back the way she had come, took a detour down another residential avenue. She was feeling strange — like someone had picked her up and dropped her in a bowl of jelly. Had being in the church put some sort of spell on her?

Jess headed back to the house. She was tired and didn't feel like walking anymore.

When she returned, Erica was in the kitchen cooking dinner. Lisah and Serena were sitting in front of the television. They didn't acknowledge Jess as she went through to her room.

Jess ran her eyes over the room. It was a picture of desolation. Everything was exactly as it had been before, but somehow it seemed worse. Books which were once bound and legible, lay crumpled and torn. Some of her homework lay in a damp patch on the carpet where a vase of Erica's flowers had been upturned. The ink had run over the paper, like tears streaked across a face. Jess picked it up. It was still limp and damp. The glass from a picture frame that had hung on the wall lay in fragments below it. The cut flowers, which had decorated the room and given it a remote touch of sanity, were crushed and trampled into the carpet. Their life had been squeezed from them and they forlornly resembled soldiers lying anonymously on a battle field, with no one to mourn them. The cord from the lamp lay like a coil of barbed wire at the foot of the bed.

Jess's eyes fell on the small china puppy that Margi had given her, in the far corner of the room. She made her way carefully through the remains of her rampage. She picked up the gold-coloured ornament which lay in two pieces, its head amputated cleanly from its body. Jess looked down at it, almost expecting it to bleed. She felt a sudden pang of regret.

Later, Jess lay in bed, thinking of the mess she'd made of everything around her — and not just her room. She'd managed to restore her dwellings to a state resembling some sort of order — or at least made it fit to sleep in. However, she couldn't sleep. Thoughts kept flashing through her mind. They were strange thoughts that she couldn't make any sense of. She found herself thinking of Mark, kicking the football on the school oval. His face was not a clear picture. The only time she'd seen it up close was her first day at school, when they'd collided. It had been embarrassed and apologetic then.

Jess lay awake, looking up at the ceiling. It seemed like a long way away in the darkness. What was really to become of her life? She wondered. It was the first time she'd looked beyond what was immediately in front of her and admitted to herself how much she actually cared.

CHAPTER 17

Her sleep had been fitful and her dreams confusing. It was now Saturday. Jess dreaded going back to school. Her crumpled school bag was the first thing she saw when she awoke, and her heart immediately sank, both at the prospect of school and the devastated room. She felt ashamed, a little like she had after she'd been drunk, but not as intensely. She struggled to bring back to her mind the feelings that made her do this.

Jess got dressed and went into the kitchen. Serena sat at the table eating her breakfast. There was no one else in the room. She eyed Jess and then looked back down at her breakfast. Was she angry at her for what Jess had said about Robert? Since Jess's return, the girls had snubbed her, even the twins. It didn't bother her. She usually had no desire to talk to them anyway. Ben was still making an effort to be friendly and continued to invite her to join in with the things he did. She hated him making a special effort. She'd rather he just be natural and cold like the rest of them.

Jess sat across from Serena at the table, purposefully close. She poured herself some cornflakes and dowsed them with milk. Suddenly she said, 'Did you really get stabbed?'

Serena looked up from her bowl. Jess examined her expression. It was calm and cautious. Her jaws went up and down slowly as she chewed on her cereal. For a moment her hazel eyes rested on Jess's face, as if seeing her for the first time.

'Who told you that?' she asked.

'Is it true?' Jess persisted.

'Did Erica say that?'

'She said you've probably had it tougher than what I have.'

There was another pause. Serena didn't respond to this bait as Jess thought she might.

'My adopted father tried to kill me once. But he couldn't. I was too tough. He hated me for telling someone what he used to do to me. I suppose she told you about that too.' There was no resentment in the girl's voice, nor arrogance.

'Was he a drunk?'

'No, just a poor deranged man. I think he's in jail now.' She said the last piece of information as if it were irrelevant. 'My mother was nice, I liked her. She died of breast cancer. She told me to look after him. That was some joke. He probably thought he was looking after *me*. I don't think about it much anymore.' Serena was looking past Jess now, at the wall or something else behind her. Jess marvelled at the lack of anger in her words and how readily she now spoke of her past.

'I guess you have had it tough …' Jess stammered feebly. Serena returned to her breakfast, mashing the soggy cereal with her spoon.

'Is Boogert your real mother's last name?' Jess inquired, unrelenting in her probing of Serena's past.

'No, it's my adopted name.'

Jess wondered how she could endure such an ever-present vestige of an unhappy life.

'What about you, why don't you live with your parents?' ventured Serena, sensing some new affiliation between them. Jess noticed that she was watching her intently. With a shake of her head she rose from her seat.

'It doesn't matter,' she said, her manner becoming distant once again.

'Why won't you talk about it?'

Jess had reverted to her silent, repressed outward demeanour.

'Why don't you tell anyone anything? Why do you have to be so secretive and mysterious all the time?' Serena demanded disapprovingly. Jess turned and walked toward the back door, as if she hadn't heard, but she had heard, and the words were corrosive to the fragile metal of her heart.

Over the weekend, Jess came down with the flu, relieving the anticipated agony of returning to school. She revelled in this temporary postponement of events. For two days she was confined to bed and for once experienced no adversity to being secluded in her room. By Wednesday however, the situation had lost most of its appeal. Jess left the house feeling depressed and apathetic. It could have been her illness, or perhaps the hollow significance of the day. It was Jess's birthday. She was fifteen, a year older and a year closer to her death. She didn't feel any desire to reflect on the last year, despite it being the most eventful of her life.

Jess's idleness took her to the park across from the pub. She found a park bench situated in the corner of the grassed area and lay down on it on her back. The headache and congestion were still gripping her. She folded her arms across her face to block out the bright sunlight that penetrated her closed eyelids. It was a very quiet spot. The only sounds were the sparrows in the trees and the occasional car engine, purring its way to its destination along the road on the other side of the park. There weren't usually any people around at that time between breakfast and midday, so Jess was startled when a voice sounded directly above her.

'Hard night, huh?'

Jess jerked her head up off the bench, and stared into the face of Mark, the footy star from the school oval, who was looking down at her with a grin. She struggled to sit up into a more commanding position and brushed the hair out of her eyes.

'Get chucked out of home, did you?' he said jovially.

'Of course not, I'm just … relaxing,' Jess said seriously. She looked self-consciously into his face. He was still grinning.

'I heard you got smashed.'

'Who told you that?' Jess felt her face burning red. She wished he hadn't heard this piece of information.

'Just a rumour going around at school.' He shrugged casually, as if it were no big deal. It was a big deal to Jess. She felt her dignity slipping out from under her.

'You shouldn't believe everything you hear,' she defended herself.

'Why don't you go to school anymore, Jess?' His stating of her name sent a shiver down her spine.

'I'm sick,' she replied.

'You don't look too sick to me,' Mark observed.

'What are you, a doctor or something?'

He smiled perplexingly. She shifted under his gaze.

'Didn't you know? I graduated when I was twelve — a child genius.' He was clearly enjoying himself.

Jess was forced into a smile. 'That's why you're doing Grade ten, right?' she said sarcastically.

'I like the company.'

Jess looked down at the grass. 'I bet Brianna and her little gang are having a ball without me,' Jess said, taking the opportunity to satisfy her curiosity and to change the subject.

'It's quite a big gang, actually, but I wouldn't worry about her, she's all hot air,' Mark dismissed Jess's rival.

She was taken in by his casual nature. 'Why aren't *you* at school?'

'I've got a free lesson.'

'Oh, right.' She didn't believe him. There was a moment's silence. 'I think I'd better be getting home,' she said. He looked at her questioningly. 'Erica will be wondering where I am,' she added. Why did she have to justify anything to him? She was angry with herself.

He didn't seem convinced but didn't try to stop her. 'I guess I'll see you at school then.'

'Yeah, maybe.'

As Jess made her way along the familiar route home, she

felt a confusing mixture of disappointment, irritation, and a prickling sensation in her chest. Just before she reached their street, she changed her direction and disappeared down into the dry creek bed where she could have a chance to think.

For the rest of the day she was restless and on edge. Mark was a total stranger to her, yet she suddenly felt as though she'd known him for years. It was strange. With a single fleeting conversation, he had invaded her solitary world, the way the psychologist, Ben, and the Pullins had not been able to do. Somehow, though, she could find no resentment inside her for this unthinkable intrusion.

Jess's return to school was an anticlimax. She'd been prepared for a barrage of curiosity about her exploits with the bottle. When the anticipated attention didn't eventuate, Jess was relieved. Accompanying this though, was a slight feeling of loneliness. Jess had never really minded being ignored before, but now the lack of attention from her peers had given her a strange and unexpected sense of inadequacy. Even Brianna had not mentioned the incident, and Jess was beginning to wonder if Mark was the only one who knew. Jess was behind in her work and she used the lunch breaks in a vain attempt to catch up, more out of necessity to occupy the empty minutes than out of devotion to her studies.

Jess changed her route to school to avoid having to pass the church, which she was convinced had been responsible for the strange confusion she'd felt these last days. The new walk was longer and less picturesque, but worth the inconvenience. There was something about that old church that made her feel inferior — an outsider.

Her birthday had slipped by, unnoticed. She didn't know if anybody knew her date of birth anymore. She'd never told anyone, except maybe her friends in primary school. Jess could remember a few names, a couple of hazy faces, but no birthdays. They wouldn't remember hers either. They had no reason to. The only other place where there was any evidence of her existence was on a small slip of paper somewhere lost in a file in the Births Deaths and Marriages offices. It seemed fitting to Jess to state these three fundamentals of life in the same phrase, or at least the first two. A new feeling had begun to creep its way to the surface. It was a sort of dissatisfied longing, almost to the stage that she believed in it.

One afternoon, Jess sat at the bench in the garage. A pot of glue was in front of her, and next to it, the broken china puppy. She blew the dust from the shiny surface and held the two pieces together. Along the broken edge there were a few tiny chips of china missing, never to be retrieved. Jess placed the head and body on the bench and pulled the cap off the glue. Upturning the bottle, she gave it a squeeze. The nozzle emitted an oozing sound along with the flow of glue. Jess swore as she quickly righted the bottle and tried to stop the pool of semi-liquid goo dripping down onto her lap.

She picked up one of the pieces and prepared to dip it into the glue. The broken white edge contrasted starkly with the gold, almost metallic appearance of the dog's outer surface. How could something be so different on the inside to the outside that everybody saw? The pure white porcelain reminded her of the statue in the church, looking down over the people.

She was suddenly snapped out of her thoughts by movement at the front of the garage. She quickly jerked her head around. Ben wheeled his bike through the door and let it fall against the wall. He looked up and saw Jess.

'What are you doing?' he asked.

'Nothing.'

Ben saw the china puppy lying on the bench. 'What happened to it?' he said, pointing.

'It broke,' Jess replied. Ben smiled, taking this statement of the obvious as friendly humour.

'How?'

'I dropped it.'

'Was it a present or something?'

'Yeah, from my last foster mum.'

'I thought you didn't like them?'

Jess shrugged her shoulders. 'Margi was okay.'

Ben didn't say anything. He simply nodded his head and reached in front of her to pick up the pieces, and examined them, one in each hand. Jess suddenly felt foolish for wanting to hang on to this relic of the past. 'Don't worry about it,' she said dismissively.

Ben ignored her and reached for the bottle of glue. Carefully, he dripped some on the raw white edges of the puppy's neck, then pressed the head onto it, lining up the edges. He wiped the excess glue away with his fingers and onto his jeans. He handed it to Jess.

'It's fast drying. It will stay there now,' he said. She put out her hand to take it.

'Thanks,' she murmured.

Ben sat down on a stool beside her.

'So, how's school going these days? I don't see you around much,' he asked.

'Okay, I guess. I'm still trying to catch up on my work at lunch times.'

Ben looked at her disbelievingly, perhaps because he doubted her dedication, or maybe he knew how long it took to catch up on four days' missed work. He played along.

'Mum would be pleased to hear that you're making an effort. She really is trying to support you, ya know.'

Jess made a face. Ben looked at her, trying to assess her feelings. His red hair was slightly ruffled, probably from the ride home in the wind, and his face was pink. His freckled face accentuated his friendliness. It perhaps helped to make him the least threatening member of the family.

'So, what's happening in the wilds of Year ten, anything exciting? Got any hot goss?' He grinned, clearly trying to make conversation.

'Not really. It's pretty dead.'

He nodded. 'Year ten was the pits. Wait 'til next year. You start getting treated like a real person — like you actually have something to contribute to the human race. The Year

Eights respect you. They move out of your way. That's the best bit. You'll be sixteen, won't you?'

'Next year, yes.' She hoped he didn't ask about her birthday.

'How's Geography going?' Ben asked, rolling his eyes slightly. He knew, as they all did, of her dislike for Mr Zelic. 'Is the old guy coping with you all right?'

'Just,' Jess replied. The truth was that their confrontations had died down lately, and Jess had been subdued in class.

'I hear that you give Zelic a real run for his money.'

Jess shrugged.

'They say you're pretty cunning.'

'Who does?' she demanded, eyeing him sharply.

'I can't remember.'

'Yes, you can.'

'A guy from your class — Mark Traicos.'

Jess raised her eyebrows. 'I didn't know he was a friend of yours,' she said.

This time Ben shrugged his shoulders. 'I didn't know he was a friend of *yours*.' He grinned again.

'He's not,' Jess snapped. 'I've just spoken to him a couple of times, that's all.'

Ben smiled knowingly.

Jess felt resentful toward his assuming manner. 'What else did he say?' she asked, unable to help herself.

'Not much really. Only that you're the most ... no, never mind.'

Jess felt hot and sweaty. She wished he would wipe that stupid grin off his face. She picked up a newspaper from the bench and threw it at him in annoyance, almost playfully.

'I've got to go and do some homework,' Ben said unconvincingly. 'I'll see you later.' He disappeared out of the garage before Jess could probe him any further.

She sat there for a while, looking down at the freshly repaired puppy, and pondering the conversation and its meaning. The confusion inside her head was raging strongly again. What was going on? Why did she feel so strange? Her insides were churning. She didn't like feeling this way. It was threatening her control over herself. For several days, a sense of restless dissatisfaction had encompassed her. Perhaps God was punishing her.

CHAPTER 18

The Bowman's frequently entertained members of their large circle of friends. At least once a week extra places were set at the table. Sometimes they were friends of the kids, but usually it was a couple or another family. Jess found it hard to keep up. She wondered whether they knew everybody in Stonewell. Jess felt uncomfortable being introduced along with the others. If one of the dinner guests attempted a conversation with her they found her unresponsive and disinterested. Sometimes she tried to make an effort, sensing Robert's eyes on her, or simply because she was tired of being the odd one out. The ones she liked most were those who didn't say anything to her at all.

One night Erica put on a Tupperware party. She asked Jess to carry drinks around to the guests.

'Why can't Lisah do it, or Serena?' Jess asked.

'Because I'm asking you.'

'I have a lot of homework to do tonight,' Jess said, then added, 'But thanks for asking anyway.' She thought Erica looked disappointed. Jess went to her room feeling despondent, but not really knowing why.

After Geography one day Mr Zelic called Jess to his desk. She wondered what she could possibly have done this time.

'I'm glad to see you've settled down in class lately. It's a pity your grades don't reflect it though,' he said. Jess had shrugged her shoulders.

'You are much too smart to be wasting your brain. You could be doing much better.'

Jess wondered why he was suddenly so concerned but didn't say anything.

It was almost October. The year was slipping by. It would soon be the holidays, then Christmas would follow, just like it did every other year. This thought made Jess realise that the world really was the same one she'd occupied last year and the year before that. The repetitiveness of the months and the seasons was a reminder of that.

Jess wondered what Christmas would be like at the Bowmans. She wondered if anyone would bother to give her anything. She could imagine the others surrounded by gifts, from friends and devoted relatives. She would be there too, with maybe a couple of gifts from Robert and Erica so that she didn't feel left out — trinkets and clothes she'd probably never wear.

She remembered her last Christmas with her parents. It was hardly worth remembering. Her father had been to the pub until late on Christmas Eve. After a run in with Jess's mother that had woken the whole street, he had set his cigarette lighter to the small pile of presents that was waiting to be opened on Christmas morning, and watched them burn on the back veranda. No one had felt very festive after that.

On the Thursday evening, a week before the end of term, they were all seated around the dinner table. There was a hum of anticipation in the air, with plans for the upcoming holidays bouncing back and forth across the table. The twins were making sculptures with their cutlery and nobody seemed to mind.

'Mum, Jacqui and Kara invited us to go bowling with them on Saturday night, is that okay?' Lisah interjected into the flood of conversation.

'Who's us?'

'Ben and Serena and I,' she replied.

'What about Jess?' Erica said.

'Oh yeah, she can come too if she wants,' Lisah said, throwing a glance briefly across the table at Jess. Jess wished Erica hadn't said anything. It they'd wanted her along Lisah would have said so.

'No thanks,' she muttered.

'Come on, it will be fun,' Ben coaxed.

'I don't want to go bowling with your stupid friends. Why don't you just leave me alone,' she shot at him. 'Stop interfering in my life. None of you know what my life is like.' After adding this last sentence, she withdrew back into herself again, for the words were a piece of her soul, now released and hanging revealingly in the air around them.

Serena, who sat directly opposite Jess, threw her fork down onto her plate. Everybody's eyes shifted from their meals to rest on her.

'Why don't you stop feeling so god-damned sorry for yourself!' she barked at Jess.

'Serena!' Erica said sharply.

'I don't care,' Serena snapped back. '*Somebody* has to tell her.' She turned back to Jess who was looking into her heated, angry face. 'We're just trying to include you in our normal things. But I forgot, you're not normal, are you? You're Jess, the one who can't even find it within herself to serve drinks at a bloody Tupperware party. You act as if the whole world's against you. You sit in your room all the time by yourself as if no one else is good enough for you. It seems like you're on another planet half the time and you expect us to take your crap and not say anything. I feel sorry for Robert and Erica the way you treat them after all they've done for you. And I'm sick of being careful all the time not to tread on your toes. Erica says you've just got to settle in. Well you've had three months to settle in. You're just a stuck up misery guts — an ungrateful little bitch!' Serena kept her eyes fixed on Jess. They were blazing. After a moment when nobody spoke, Serena rose from her seat, squeezed past Robert, and ran from the dining room. Jess glanced at Ben. His face was flushed a deep crimson red. His expression made her feel worthless.

Jess lay awake on top of the quilt on her bed for a long time that night, a deluge of thoughts going around in her head, threatening to make her dizzy. Would anyone ever understand her? Would she ever understand herself? Why did she care whether anyone did or not, or what they thought? *I've never needed anybody*, she thought, *and I don't need anybody now*. How could she let someone like Serena bother her?

For hours she lay there. She heard everybody go to bed. The house was silent and dark. Jess might as well have been the only person in the world just then. Questions kept flowing continually into her consciousness, questions she couldn't answer. Why was she so different to everybody else?

Without being able to help it, things Serena had said kept going through her mind — the accusations, sharp and penetrating. She had been right about one thing. The whole world was against her. She was alone. She wasn't feeling sorry for herself — or if she was, she had reason to. She didn't treat Robert and Erica badly — except maybe that once ... One thing she was certain of was that she wasn't ungrateful — or perhaps only sometimes. She was becoming less and less sure about anything.

Lying in the pitch darkness into the night, the only sound was her breathing, rhythmic and forced, keeping her alive, perhaps against her will. She remembered the night she'd been drunk. There were similarities between then and tonight. But just exactly what she couldn't put her finger on. Jess thought long and hard about the way she was then and the way she was now.

The realisation washed over her so that it was almost a physical experience. Everything Serena had said — it was all true! But it was the only way she knew. She had thought she was free, independent and superior. Other people simply got in the way of her illusions and threatened to break them down. The admittance was a relief, more so than she could have imagined. What a burden it was constantly trying to uphold this self-image. She was just wallowing in self-pity. She said these things over and over to herself, until the emotional exhaustion eventually overcame her, and she faded into sleep. That night she slept more soundly than perhaps she ever had in her life.

'What are you doing?' Ben came into the room and sat down on the floor.

'Just reading some of these trashy magazines that Lisah left out,' Jess said, holding up the cover of one of them, containing a full page glossy photograph of a fake-looking model, smiling out at them. 'I never realised how much garbage some people write.'

'Yeah, I know what you mean.'

'I didn't know you were into this stuff?' She made a face.

'Think I'm desperate or something?'

'You'd have to be.'

'I know what would be more fun than sitting around here reading that stuff,' Ben said, sensing a certain uncharacteristic lightness about her mood.

'What?' Jess asked suspiciously.

'There's a drop-in night at the youth club tonight,' Ben said tentatively.

'Really?' Jess could see that he was watching her reaction, so tried not to let her face show anything at all.

'Yeah, it'll be good. Real casual. There will be people you know there.'

Jess sat silently looking at him.

'And it's only two blocks away, so you can come home any time you like.'

'Okay.'

Ben sat up straight, as if someone had just struck him in the face. 'Okay? You'll come?'

'Yeah, that's what I said.'

'Great, let's go then,' he grinned, getting up before she could change her mind. 'Do you need to get ready or anything?'

'No, I'm fine the way I am.' Jess rose to her feet, kicking the magazines aside.

As they walked down the street, side by side, Jess wondered what she had gotten herself into. She was not sure just exactly why she'd agreed to go. She remembered Ben's reaction. Was she really that predictable?

They reached the youth club which was a large rendered brick building surrounded by lawn. The entrance faced the creek. Jess had been past it but hadn't been inside. Music thumped its way through the walls. Jess followed Ben inside. She glanced quickly around her, taking everything in. There were people standing around talking. Six people were sharing a couch. There was a group of guys around an eight-ball table, entertained by an absorbing contest between two of them whom she knew from school. They were all throwing advice and strategy suggestions at the two players.

Ben wandered over to the drinks bar. Jess followed him. He started talking to somebody, and Jess finished scanning the room. Most of the people she'd seen at school but didn't know who all of them were. She sat down on a stool by the bar. A girl from Jess's English class walked over to her, towing her boyfriend by the hand.

'Hi Jess. I haven't seen you here before. This is cool, isn't it? You know Will, don't you? Hey, how did you go in that last essay we had to do? It was really dumb, wasn't it?'

'Do we have to talk about *that*?' Will said.

'He failed,' the girl said grandly, as if it were a world headline. Will didn't flinch. Jess could see who wore the shoes in their relationship. For a while the girl (whom Jess thought was called Cassy or Cathy or something like it) chatted on, asking Jess questions, but not pausing for a reply. Jess simply nodded and tried to listen to what she was saying. She glanced around for Ben and saw him talking to a girl in the corner. She looked around. Everyone seemed to be having a good time. Another girl dragged Will and Cassy away and Jess was now by herself. She tried to look relaxed, despite every muscle in her body being tense. She wondered again why she'd come. Perhaps to prove a point, but to herself or to others? She felt out of place among these happy, carefree teenagers. But that was nothing new.

'Do you want a drink?' Ben appeared behind her.

'No thanks — yeah, all right.' She needed to wash the lump down her throat. He returned a moment later and handed Jess a Coke.

'See, this is okay, isn't it?'

'Yeah, I guess.' She tried to manage a smile.

'Come over here and talk to the gang.'

Jess followed him to a small group in the corner where he'd been. They greeted her warmly, as if she was their good friend. Suddenly a thought came to her — what if Ben had told them he was bringing her, and that she'd refused all his other invitations. Maybe they were making a special effort for her. This made her angry.

Her eyes drifted over the room again, then stopped at the group around the pool table. There was Mark, joking with the other guys. He always fitted in so well. She heard Ben's voice, 'Why don't you …' His eyes followed her gaze. 'Why don't you go and talk to him?' he said.

'Why would I want to do that?' she said quickly, eyeing Ben sharply.

'Because he likes you.'

She glanced over at Mark again. He caught her eye and Jess felt herself blush. He smiled at her, then turned back to his mates.

'No,' she said to Ben.

For a while she stood around with Ben's friends, feeling restless. Once, she looked over in Mark's direction, and then away again. Part of her was surprised he hadn't tried to talk to her. She excused herself and escaped to the ladies room. She stood there, looking in the mirror, critically studying the face she saw in it. It was calm and expressionless, and perhaps slightly drawn. She wondered whether other people saw it the way she did. After examining it for a few more minutes, she went back into the main room. Perhaps it was time she went. Ben should be satisfied. She'd stayed quite a while. Just as she started towards the door, she heard a voice behind her.

'Jess.'

She turned around to look at Mark.

'Are you having fun?' he asked.

'I suppose,' she managed.

'Do you want to go outside?' he continued.

Jess's heart leapt. What was he planning to do? 'I don't know,' she said helplessly, looking around for Ben. She couldn't see him.

'Come on,' he coaxed. 'You can trust me.' There was none of the previous humour in his voice. Reluctantly, Jess followed him out of the club, not knowing what else to do. Mark walked to the edge of the grass and leaned on the railing overlooking the creek. The moon was out, glistening on the shallow water below them, which was interrupted by stones and clumps of weeds. The air was not as cold as it had been a few weeks ago. The September night hinted of the approaching summer. The dull thudding bass notes of the music still reached them, but the night was comparatively peaceful to the crowded club. Jess pushed aside the hair that the slight breeze blew across her face. She waited for Mark to say something, but he kept gazing across the creek. She stood silently, watching his contoured, angular face, which seemed to glow in the moonlight. Finally, he turned to face her.

'I'm glad you came tonight,' he said. 'I had a feeling you might.'

Jess narrowed her eyes, suddenly becoming suspicious again. 'Have you been talking to Ben?' she asked.

'This has nothing to do with Ben.'

She shifted uneasily. *What has it got to do with then?* was the question that burned on her lips, but she dared not ask it, for she was afraid of the answer.

'I've never met anyone like you, Jess. You're just different to all the other girls I've known.'

'Yeah? And how's that?'

'I don't know. You're just more … more real.'

Her head buzzed with confusion over the ambiguity of his statement.

'You have guts. You're not afraid to tell people what you think,' he continued.

Jess stood still, as if anchored to the spot. Even in the near darkness, she could feel his eyes drilling through her.

'You're mysterious. That's what I like about you — never know what you're going to do next.'

Why did he have to talk about her like this? She became aware of her heart pounding relentlessly against her chest. She didn't feel fear. It was like he had her under a bewitching spell. Mark turned to look back over the creek. He was so confident and self-assured. She almost resented it.

'What are you thinking about?' Mark asked, as if he was an actor in a romance movie. Jess wondered how many times he had done this before. She didn't say anything. Perhaps she didn't want to reveal her true thoughts, or maybe she couldn't have spoken if she'd tried.

'I wouldn't even want to try to guess,' he said with a captivating smile. Jess looked at the ground. Taking a step closer, Mark reached toward her, but Jess had already moved away. His hand brushed lightly over the back of hers, and she felt a wave of panic, and something else she couldn't identify. Mark stood where he was, looking at her.

'Um, I think I should be going home,' Jess said, almost in a whisper. She waited for him to say something, but he just gazed at her. Jess turned, and slowly began to walk back toward the footpath. When she reached it, she stole a glance behind her. Mark was still standing there, his hands in his pockets, watching her walk away. Her heart sank slightly. She stepped onto the concrete path and walked quickly down the road.

The confusion began to race inside her head again. She was caught between two sets of feelings — one telling her she should go away and never look at him again, and the other drawing her back. Mark was bringing what was on the inside to the outside, where it was exposed and vulnerable. The conflict of emotions threatened to overpower her. She hated the feeling. She fought against it, but it was unrelenting.

The red flashing lights flickered over the footpath and reflected off the wet, gleaming road. The police car was pulled over on the other side of the road, and an ambulance blocked the view of the crumpled vehicle against the lamp pole.

Jess walked along the footpath a little further until the scene was in full view. She stood still, watching, almost hiding, as if should someone see her they would send her away. Paramedics in uniform hurried about the scene with a sense of urgency. The sound of muffled voices talking into two-way radios and someone barking out commands reached her. A policeman wearing a reflective vest stood behind the ambulance, ready to direct any traffic away from the horrific scene. There was no traffic though. The road, for as far as Jess could see in either direction, was deserted. There were no houses along Battersby Road. She wondered why they hadn't heard the sirens from the club, then realised the noise inside would have drowned out anything one and a half blocks away.

She crouched down on the sidewalk and watched the frenzy of activity. When an ambulance officer moved in her direction, she backed behind the trees. Looking at the wrecked car properly now for the first time, she could make out a face resting against the window. She shuddered and wondered whether the person was dead or alive. The light of the street lamp falling on the pale skin made it seem ghost-like.

Somebody moved in her line of sight, and a loud rasping sound told her they were cutting away the metal with some kind of electric saw. For several minutes they worked, trying to free the victim or victims. The windscreen of the brown sedan was smashed and lying in fragments across the road. The whole car seemed to have been crushed to half its original length against the post. Jess heard a cry of pain. It sounded like a girl. For a while Jess could not see what they were doing as there were paramedics crowded around the driver's side of the vehicle, which was facing her. She could hear voices talking to whoever was inside, and an occasional strangled cry. The sound made Jess's blood curdle.

Finally, they backed away from the car, enabling somebody to lift the girl onto a low stretcher. She looked to Jess to be about seventeen or eighteen. Her jeans were ripped, and streaks of blood glistened on her skin in the light from the ambulance headlights. They crowded around her again, and Jess strained her eyes to see. The girl again began to cry out — it sounded like somebody's name.

Someone was now working on the other side of the car. Another stretcher was wheeled to the passenger door. When the shadows momentarily shifted, Jess could just make out another figure inside. They seemed to linger over the second person for a long time. The first stretcher was wheeled into the back of the ambulance. Jess caught a glimpse of the face. The features were pulled into a grimace that was apparent even from where she was sitting. The girl had short brown hair that fell over her face, possibly hiding still more emotion. Her head dropped back onto the stretcher. An ambulance officer climbed in behind her.

Jess sat frozen to the spot as the second stretcher was wheeled away from the car, covered from head to foot by a white sheet. She could make out the contours of the body beneath it. The cries of the person's companion intensified as the stretcher was lifted in beside her. She heard the door slam shut and in a few moments the ambulance was gone. The police seemed to linger for a long time, talking to each other in low grave voices.

In her mind Jess could see another face, lying lifeless on the cold road. There must have been blood, although she hadn't actually been allowed to see the body. The night her brother died in a motorcycle accident had been pieced together, partly from memory, partly from imagined details, to a point where she didn't know which was which. He had been eighteen, about the same age as the girl in the car. That night was like a fragmented dream now. She'd been glad at the time to be spared the worst of it. But since then she had wondered what would have been worse, the reality, stark and forceful but fixed, or the images her mind conjured up, oscillating from one gruesome possibility to the next. He was alive before her now, with his ruffled hair and youthful grin. She could almost hear him talking to her: 'What's up Gypsy Girl?' Is that what she was — a gypsy — someone destined to spend her life as a wanderer from place to place, not belonging anywhere in particular? Maybe in a physical sense or something more figurative; but in any case, unable to tell her own fortune or to have any idea of what her destiny held.

Jess walked home in a trance. It probably took a few minutes, but later she couldn't remember it. When she reached the front yard, she stopped and turned to look behind her, down the quiet street. It was still deserted. No sign of the accident was visible from their street. It was as though it had happened in another world. Breathing out slowly, she sat down on the low brick wall which bordered the yard. She closed her eyes. She could see the bright lights, pulsating as red as blood behind her eyelids, penetrating the blackness. Scrunching her eyes together more tightly, they became only brighter, blinding her. She let her eyes fall open again, pondering the scene she had just witnessed. She consciously brought the sight of the body and the tragic cries back into her mind. It was as though she was forcing herself to relive it in order to exorcise some sort of ghost. There was something about this accident that spooked her more than anything she'd encountered during her time on the streets. She'd been by herself then, away from all other human anguish. She had been the sole troubled person in the world. Now there were others, and her plight was becoming more and more insignificant in comparison, and the self-pity seemed no longer as justified.

The accident had jolted something inside her. It wasn't the brutal way that the two peoples' lives were torn apart that haunted her, for even her brother's death had triggered a greater shock and numbness than grief. But rather, it was the suddenness by which life could be terminated. What if it had been her in that car? What if she died today? It wasn't until just then that the thought that death could really come at any moment sunk into her ravaged mind. She had once thought that an end to her life would be the greatest relief. But what would be left? A trail of scars wherever she'd been and people who'd come and gone from her life, none of them better for the experience. Why should she care what happened after she was gone? But she did. There were things that would remain. There were Serena's accusations. There was Mark. He was a constant image in her mind. He was venturing into the unknown territory which was her heart.

From behind her, Jess heard a voice calling, 'Jess, are you coming inside?' It was Erica. Jess didn't know how long she'd been sitting there, but it felt late. Slowly she rose and turned toward the house.

Even long after she'd gone to bed, Jess couldn't rid the thoughts of the accident from her mind. She had taken her life's continuity for granted, even if it was a miserable continuity. She shuddered away from the thought of her life ending the way it was. The memory of when she'd almost ended it came back to her. She hadn't thought about it in weeks. She thought of her body imprisoned in a dark wooden coffin, helpless to change anything. She saw the ruins lying around her grave. Jess wasn't certain about many things, but one thing she was certain of was that she didn't want to remain the way she was.

Jess's resolution brought her to the breakfast table early the next morning — Saturday morning. She waited for Robert to sit down with his newspaper. She was afraid of what she was about to do, but she knew it was the only thing to do.

As Robert took his seat he glanced over at Jess, sitting upright with her arms folded on the edge of the table, apparently calm. Her eyes met his.

'Hello,' he said.

'Hi,' Jess replied. Robert rested his eyes on her expectantly for several seconds, then turned back to his newspaper.

'I'm sorry,' Jess said coolly, not wanting him to know how difficult this was to do. Robert looked up at her again, intently this time.

'What for?' He looked confused.

'Those things I said about you.' Jess checked for his reaction. His face was blank, so she continued, 'At the police station, saying you'd molested me. I shouldn't have said it.' Her face fell so that she didn't see his expression, but she could imagine it. She traced the pattern of the tablecloth with her finger and waited for Robert to say something.

At first, he said nothing, then, 'Jess, I don't know what to say. I—'

'I'm sorry,' Jess repeated.

'I believe you. I think you *are* sorry. Thank you.'

Jess could sense the surprise and elation in his voice. She thought she'd feel good, but she didn't. She felt worthless and ashamed. She continued, trying to ease her guilt.

'I shouldn't have used you to get what I wanted and I'm sorry for humiliating you.'

Robert nodded, but seemed puzzled about where this sudden rush of humility had come from. They looked at each other in silence for a moment. Jess noticed for the first time that Robert had a scar over his left eyebrow.

Jess's outward calmness continued. 'I guess I've been sorry since I dropped the charges,' she said revealingly.

Robert smiled. 'Jess, despite what you may think of yourself, you really do have a lot of things going for you. You've proven that just now. You have guts, and a soft heart deep down.'

Jess remembered Mark saying almost the same thing.

Robert's face relaxed for a moment into a smile. 'You've been forced to make decisions that other people your age wouldn't even dream of. I think it's strengthened you and you've grown up a lot — even since you've been here, whether you feel like it or not. You know, hidden inside somewhere there really is a great person.'

Jess sat silently, listening. Normally Robert's words would have unsettled her, but they no longer stung like they once would have.

'Am I right in saying that it was what you wanted to do to your own father, and that taking it out on me was some kind of partial revenge?'

Jess sunk back into her chair. She hadn't thought about it like that before, but it made sense.

'My father was a drunk. He hated me.' She hadn't

spoken about her parents to anyone since that day in Olivia's bedroom.

'I can't imagine what that would be like,' Robert sympathised.

'My mum mostly acted like I wasn't there. They never wanted a second kid.' A tear slid down her cheek and dropped onto her collarbone. She sat silently, looking down at the table. If Robert felt the urge to comfort her by offering a shoulder to cry on, he resisted. Perhaps he knew more of what was going on inside her head than she thought.

Just then Ben walked into the kitchen. He stopped when he saw them. He looked at Jess's face. Without saying anything, he tactfully retreated to the living room. Jess used the disruption to regain her composure. She pushed her chair back and stood up. She walked towards the door.

'Thanks for the chat,' Robert called after her.

'Can I open it now?'

'In a minute Honey. Where are the serviettes?'

'I think they're still in the kitchen.'

'Pleeeeeaaaase can I open it now?'

'I said in a minute, Kate. Why don't we cut the cake first?'

'Sounds good to me.'

'All you ever think about is your stomach, Ben.'

The clamour of activity and the flood of voices filled the dining room. The family was crowded around the big table which was piled with food. A large cake, with eight candles and swirls of vanilla cream deposited generously over it, sat in the centre of the table. It was the twins' birthday. Everyone seemed in great spirits that evening.

'What kind of cake is it?'

'Black forest.'

'Ooh yum.'

'Can somebody go and get the matches please?'

'Hurry up. I'm starving.'

'Shut up Ben, anyone would think that half a roast chicken and four baked potatoes would be enough for you.'

'Can we open the presents now?'

'Soon, okay? Have we got the matches?'

Erica lit the candles on the cake. The flames danced and flickered in the air, disturbed by the activity around them. The words of *Happy Birthday* filled the dining room, some slightly out of tune, each person adding his or her own individual touch to the traditional song. Ginger and Kate tussled with each other, vying for the best vantage point to blow out the candles.

'I got the most.'

'No you didn't. I got that one over the other side.'

'You're both just a couple of wind bags,' Robert teased. Both girls collapsed into a fit of giggles.

Jess took her piece of cake from Erica as it was passed across the table. She eyed the dark brown wedge-shaped slice. She hadn't joined in singing *Happy Birthday*, but she didn't think anyone had noticed. They were probably more likely to have noticed if she *had* joined in. Jess sat in silence as she did for most of the meals. She had nothing to say — no reason to complain. Erica was a good cook. Jess attacked the cake with her fork.

'Can we open the presents now?'

'Finish your cake.'

The twins' eagerness and exuberance intrigued Jess. She couldn't remember birthdays being like this at home.

'I've finished.'

'Okay, you can open them.' As soon as Erica had conceded this permission, Ginger and Kate flew into action, tearing the paper from the numerous presents piled between them. One advantage of having a large family was that there were always plenty of presents. The table became cluttered with toys and gadgets made to amuse eight-year-old girls. The last unopened parcel lay on the table, amid the cake crumbs and torn wrapping paper.

'Who's going to open it?' asked Robert.

'Me,' both Ginger and Kate chorused.

'Who's it from?' Kate asked.

'It's from all of us,' Erica answered.

'Even Jess?'

'Yes of course. She's part of the family.'

Jess, who had been sitting silently, watching, moved uncomfortably in her chair. Several faces threw an uneasy glance in her direction, then drifted back to the twins. Kate, apparently satisfied with this reply, proceeded to tear the wrapping from the parcel, but Ginger looked her mother solemnly in the eye.

'No she isn't.'

'What makes you say that, sweetheart?' Erica said. Ginger continued, unfazed and as if Jess were not in the room.

'Cos she wasn't born here.'

'Neither was Serena,' Erica replied, with a gesture of her hand which indicated to finish opening the present and dismiss the subject. But Ginger wasn't satisfied.

'That's different. Serena is nice and doesn't act weird.'

The colour began to rise in Erica's cheeks and she looked apologetically across the table at Jess. Jess had sat listening to the conversation. The table had fallen completely silent. She noticed everyone looking at her, almost expectantly, and even thought she detected a glimmer of fear in Serena's evasive gaze. Jess's face remained expressionless. They were all waiting for her to say something. What were they expecting — some angry retort, or a bitter indulgence in self-pity?

She sat still for a moment more, remembering the last time she'd been the centre of a dinner table confrontation. Serena had cracked, and Jess had given in to her assault by not responding. She had allowed the accusations to be cultivated, unrefuted, in the minds of the others at the table. No, this time would be different. Jess sat up a little straighter in her chair and slowly opened her mouth to speak. Then finally the words came flowing out.

'It's okay. She's had plenty of reasons to think that. I don't really blame her.' She turned to the younger twin. 'I know Serena will always mean more to you than I will, but can you at least give me a chance?' The last part of the sentence was directed not only at Ginger but to all of them and they seemed

to sense it. Jess knew they had given her many chances —
more than she deserved. It was almost as if it was a statement
of her intentions rather than a plea for a final chance. Jess
spoke slowly and purposefully as if to make sure the words
came out the right way. 'The present wasn't really from me.
That was just Robert and Erica denying the way things really
are — were,' she stated philosophically, the result of many
hours of self-deliberation.

Jess looked individually at the face of each member of the
Bowman family. They all conveyed a similar expression of
subdued thoughtfulness. She thought she even saw a hint of
guilt in some of their eyes. Nobody said a word. Jess couldn't
stand the atmosphere any longer.

'Well,' she said suddenly, 'why don't you finish opening
that present, I'm dying to see what it is.' As soon as she'd said
this, a smile broke out on Erica's face and everyone seemed to
relax. After a few moments, the attention was focused again
on the twins. Jess's heart was still pounding but she felt an
enormous gush of relief. She didn't know it could make her
feel so good.

Towards the end of the meal, Jess noticed that Serena was
watching her from across the table. As their eyes met, Serena
didn't look away as she had so often in the past, but her face
softened into a smile. Had Jess just imagined it, or was it a
smile of acceptance?

CHAPTER 20

Jess didn't see Mark again alone until the following Thursday. She had left the house late that morning. The school bell had rung fifteen minutes before she'd arrived. She bustled into the corridor and almost ran into him as she flew past. She made her way around him and over to the second block of lockers.

'Fancy meeting you here,' Mark said.

'Yeah, fancy.' Why did she always have to answer with such short, stunted replies? What was she guarding, the jewels of her heart?'

Mark moved swiftly to her side. 'Jess,' he said.

'What?'

There was a slight pause before he spoke. He looked down at her hand, trying to turn the key in the lock.

'That's not your locker.'

She quickly withdrew the key, embarrassed, and placed it in the locker alongside. The door opened easily.

'Jess,' he repeated. She looked at him, aware of something dancing in those magnetic eyes. 'What would you say if I asked you to go out with me?' He studied her reaction. Jess felt herself beginning to sweat. She swallowed a lump in her throat.

'But ... you're so popular ... and—' she stammered weakly.

'And you're so beautiful.'

Jess shook her head. 'You don't want to date me.'

'I know what I want.'

Jess shifted on the spot. 'The bell is about to go,' she said feebly, glancing at the clock in the hallway.

'Let it.'

Jess started to feel dizzy. It was as though she was encapsulated in a glass cylinder, unable to move.

'What are you scared of?'

Jess didn't reply. He was very close to her now, his chest almost touching her shoulder. She felt his hand find her fingers, squeezing them. Her own hand lingered for a brief moment, before she instinctively pulled it away. But it was long enough.

They both jumped as the shrill sound of the bell, signalling the beginning of the first lesson, intruded sharply into their fortress. Mark moved away from her.

'Think about it,' he said, before disappearing into the classroom, leaving Jess standing in the corner of the locker room, mulling over Mark's words and her own confused feelings.

It was a pleasant morning, calm with just a tinge of warmth in the air. Jess pushed the white lace curtain aside with the pen she held in her hand. She leaned closer to the window. The front garden was immaculate as usual. Erica spent many hours making sure of that. There was no traffic, no birds, no distractions, no nothing — perfectly conducive to study.

Why then couldn't she concentrate? Jess glanced down at the Maths book that lay on her lap, its front cover folded back over the spine. The numbers and symbols seemed to blur into each other. She let the curtain fall against the window and reclined back in the arm chair she was sitting in.

The Bowman's had gone to a local community event that morning. Jess had stayed home, planning to spend the weekend catching up on school work. It was perhaps the first time she'd planned anything for months, but it wasn't working the way she had hoped. She thought maybe it would take her mind off Mark, but she could think of nothing else. Why did he have to complicate things? What was she going to do? Things were getting out of control. She had never felt quite so confused. She didn't know what she really felt — if indeed she felt anything. So many things had changed over the last few weeks. She didn't know if it was herself or everyone else who was different. Nothing felt the same. In a way it was a relief, and in another, it was terrifying.

Jess kept hearing Mark's voice inside her head: *'What are you scared of?'* He was different — so different. Somehow, he made her feel like a real human being. He appreciated her individuality, not just assumed he knew what was going on inside her head like everyone else. He wasn't forceful or demanding like the others she'd known. It was as if he actually understood her. One question kept going around and around in her head: *Why would he be interested in me?* If she wasn't worthy of her parents' love, how could she be worthy of anyone else's? Mark must have been motivated by some other force, something sinister. She couldn't bring herself to believe that either. She felt helpless to suppress the confusion that she felt. She wanted to scream out, but there was no one to hear. There was nothing but her sullen thoughts to keep her company. But that was usually the way it was. Solitude was easy. It was safe. The fear of being hurt overrode the loneliness. All her life, people had been rejecting her, passing her on to somebody else. What assurance did she have that it wouldn't happen again?

Jess realised she'd been staring out the window. There was now a car parked across the street. She hadn't seen it arrive. She looked back down at her Maths book, which had now slid down to her knees and threatened to topple off. She couldn't even see the writing on the page, as the room seemed almost dark after looking out into the bright sunlight.

Jess couldn't bear the tedium of sitting still any longer. She rose from the chair. The text book fell to the floor and flipped shut. She walked into the kitchen, then down the hall to the bathroom. Even in the dim light, her untidy hair looked a sight in the mirror. She ran her fingers through it, vowing that Mark would never see her like this. But what did it matter? Jess leaned against the wash basin for support. Why should he be doing this to her? The anger rippled through her. But it wasn't Mark's fault the way she felt. How could it be? It had nothing to do with him — no — it had everything to do with him. Jess wondered whether anyone else ever felt the way she did just then, or whether it was her own private hell, isolated from everyone and everything. Every part of her was in conflict, with itself and the things she didn't dare to feel. She was back in the living room now. She found herself wondering again if there really was a God. Did anybody really know? Somehow though, she felt for certain now that there was.

What a mess she and others had made of her life. But they hadn't killed her spirit. Nobody could do that. She thought of all the people in her life she had shunned. No not all. That was too many to remember. Were people really not worth having, or was she just afraid of getting hurt? It was a chance she'd just have to take.

As she stood in the doorway leading from the kitchen to the living room, her heartbeat seemed to slow to a protracted murmur. It had found a new rhythm. The voices in her head were silent. She stood there, embracing the doorframe for at least half an hour, but it was as if no time had passed. The realisation came in a slow relieving wave. It had always been this way. But only now could she accept it.

As Jess left the house she shivered with excitement. She flicked the dead-lock into place and walked down the sloping lawn to the curb. Her head felt light as she made her way purposefully down the street. For once she felt like she was taking control. It was a wonderful, indescribable feeling. She was only fifteen. She most likely had years ahead of her — years that would be filled with life, not just existence, making up for the last decade and a half.

She knew where he lived. Ben had pointed out the house

to her one day. She felt like she already knew the route. She stopped for a moment in front of the large house, which had bay windows that stood out from the level of the front door. It seemed so quiet and still. Her body tingled. Walking towards the door, she wondered vaguely what she would do if he wasn't home, but the thought vanished in the air. She had come this far; no dissenting thoughts would intrude now.

The doorbell rang, resounding throughout the house, reminding her of the church bell. Now there was no turning back. She stared at the door handle. It turned. She lifted her head to see the face that was in front of her.

'Jess!' The syllable stood out like a pillar of stone.

Mark looked at her through the screen door. He seemed not quite sure what to expect.

'Can I come in?' She heard herself say. He opened the door. Jess stepped into the cool air-conditioned hallway.

'You're the last person I expected to see,' he exclaimed. 'Are you all right?'

'I will be.'

Mark fixed his eyes softly on her. He didn't need to speak. Jess gazed imploringly up at him, as if in advertisement of her feelings. Mark moved closer to her. His eyes were like no others she'd known or dared to look into. They were a deep swirling blue. She held her breath. He reached out to take her hand once again. She stiffened slightly at his touch, but this time did not pull away. She could feel the heat of his hand penetrating into her skin. Jess's insides were still turbulent, but for the first time it was not a bad feeling. Mark held her close to him. Her world-weary head fell onto his shoulder. She didn't know another human being could make her feel so safe. He didn't try to kiss her, but just soaked in the warmth of her body. How he understood her. It was as though he was an angel sent by God. There was something out there for her. She would find it.

Almost as if right on cue, he said gently, 'You'll be okay now.'

She raised her head to look at him.

'I know,' she said under her breath. 'I know.'

www.ingramcontent.com/pod-product-compliance
Lightning Source LLC
Chambersburg PA
CBHW031010190726
48286CB00003BA/781